ELLEN BOORAEM

RIVER MAGIC

DIAL BOOKS FOR YOUNG READERS

DIAL BOOKS FOR YOUNG READERS
An imprint of Penguin Random House LLC, New York

First published in the United States of America
by Dial Books for Young Readers, an imprint of
Penguin Random House LLC, 2021

Visit us online at penguinrandomhouse.com.

Library of Congress Cataloging-in-Publication Data is available.
Printed in the United States of America
ISBN 9780525428046

1 3 5 7 9 10 8 6 4 2

Design by Jason Henry • Text set in Griffo Classico

For Kathy Dawson and
Kate Schafer Testerman,
whose brilliance is matched
only by their patience

CONTENTS

CHAPTER ONE

Annabelle's Guide

The river is wide and calm in front of our house, like it never meant you any harm. But you hear the rapids all the time a quarter mile around the bend. Here's what those rapids are telling you: Do not mess with this river.

Mim—that's what we call our mom—she wanted to move away from the river after what happened to Annabelle, but we never did it. Annabelle was Mim's big sister, always lived in Maine—about always lived with us—and she loved this river. We'd be leaving her behind if we ran away.

The river being across the road is why Mim and my dad bought this house in the first place. When my dad left—just before I was born—Annabelle moved in to help out, and a few years later she and Mim started ripping stuff down and adding on and you should see it, it's amazing, everything built in like it's a boat.

Annabelle carved fruits and vegetables and animals in the woodwork, and in surprise places like inside the bookshelf. You pull out *Peterson's Field Guide to Birds* and, whoa, there's a nest of sparrows.

She painted the ceilings: a sunset in the living room, the constellation Ursa Major over my bed—that's the one with the Big Dipper, and it glows in the dark. Everywhere you look, there's Annabelle having a blast.

On May 8, eight months after Annabelle drowned, I started hearing her voice in my head.

I got a thirty-six in vocabulary that day, even though I tried real hard, and I was lying on my bed after school all miserable and sorry and listening to the rapids gurgle and *sploosh*, and I said right out loud, "Annabelle, where are you?" Because she used to help me study and when that didn't work we made brownies.

I got this buzzy feeling and there was Annabelle's voice in my head, almost like it came out of the rapids, except it was sweet and smooth, calm like deep water. Here's what she said: *Keep your tools sharp and oiled. Floss your teeth. Hello, Donna.*

"Annabelle," I whispered. "Is this you?"

Of course it's me. Jeez'm, who else?

I almost cried, except I didn't because I'd totally lose it once I got started. "I miss you. Where are you?"

Never mind that. Feeling anxious? Rub lavender oil on your temples.

That last thing was right out of Annabelle's Guide to Everyday Household Mechanics. It was a big blue loose-leaf notebook with 278 pages—except pages 115 to 118 were missing, which makes 274. Annabelle kept it in the kitchen, and it was full of recipes and instructions and advice, even poetry. I was into the Guide all the time now, trying to do chores Mim didn't have time for.

So I was sure it was my own head talking. Man, I wanted that voice to be Annabelle.

You're fine. You're smart. Not everybody's good at language arts. Which Annabelle used to tell me a lot, so those words would be in my head too. Never heard them from anybody else—Mim didn't talk about feelings too much and my big sister Janice . . . she had nothing good to say about me anymore.

Everybody should have an Annabelle. She had bright blue eyes and white hair she got when she was thirty-five, and she was little and sturdy like Mim and me, and gave amazing hugs. She taught me rope knots and knitting and woodworking, also how to get calm by doing stuff with your hands, which is like Mim and now it's like me.

Annabelle's voice started showing up every night to drift me asleep.

"Annabelle," I whispered. "I'm going to pretend this is really you."

Good plan.

Losing Annabelle changed a lot of things.

When she and Mim were kids, they had to move in with their rich cousin Betty's parents because their dad was let go from his job. Annabelle always said Cousin Betty made them feel small for being poor. After Annabelle died, Mim was in the same situation all over again because of the loans she and Annabelle took out so Mim could leave her desk job—she's a carpenter supervisor up to the university. They wanted to start their own carpentry business—well, Annabelle did, and she talked Mim into it. They bought tools and a shiny red truck, and I got to help them build a workshop out back. Mim was supposed to quit her job after Labor Day.

But Annabelle died the end of August. Mim already remortgaged the house by then, and even with the extra work she took on there was no way to keep up with all the bills. She even dropped the insurance on the red truck, which meant we couldn't use it anymore

So now Mim wanted to send *me* to live with Cousin Betty, plus her Evil Boy Twins. For the *whole summer.*

At their ugly house in Southern Maine, on a pond full of leeches.

Every video chat all winter, Cousin Betty kept saying I should come babysit the twins so she could concentrate on her mail-order bug spray business. Mim said sending your kids to live with relatives is what you do when times get tough.

She liked to say she got strong when she was a kid because of Cousin Betty being so mean, and that's why she succeeded in a man's profession. She said Cousin Betty's grown out of her meanness, mostly.

I didn't care. The one time I met Cousin Betty in person, Evil Boy Twin Andrew gave me chocolate that turned out to be Ex-Lax, plus I got a leech on me.

I really needed to stay home.

Okay, so I was hearing my dead aunt in my head. But then things got even weirder, because a lady named Vilma Bliksem moved into Mrs. Wittingham's house uphill from us. She was odd, we could tell from the start. Then she kept getting odder and odder until . . .

Well, better start at the beginning.

I found out about the new neighbor at breakfast, about a week after I started hearing Annabelle's voice. Janice was eating a thing of yogurt and Mim was packing up her briefcase and she said, "Dana at the store tells me the Wittingham kids rented their mom's house to some lady. Don't know her name." Mrs. Wittingham was old, and she died about a month after Annabelle.

"Didn't even have a moving van," Janice said, because she's in high school and knows everything. "Dave Pelletier sold her a car. She didn't have one of those either."

Janice had on blaze-orange lipstick to match her hair dye. She kept lapping her yogurt spoon real, real slow so Mim could see the stud in her tongue and get ooged out all over again. Janice is this amazing student but now she said she wasn't going to college because we couldn't afford it anyways and instead she was going to get a job and a whole bunch of tattoos.

Janice is why we call our mother "Mim"—when she was little she said it instead of "Mom" and Annabelle thought it was awful cute, so it stuck.

"Drat. Drat." Mim poked around in her briefcase, making a mess, panicking even, looking for something.

"Bus pass is here." I opened the drawer where I put it after she got home Friday.

"There it is. Thanks, Girlie-cue." Mim stuck the pass in her pocket, where it would probably get lost all over again. I didn't say anything even though it was only halfway through May and we couldn't afford two bus passes in one month.

"*Bus pass is here,*" Janice said in a squeaky, Donna-mocking voice. "What a sad little person you are."

I didn't understand why saving the bus pass made you a sad little person, but there was no talking to Janice when she was in that kind of a mood, which was pretty much every day since Annabelle died. Especially after Mim stopped paying our cell phone bills.

Mim went to catch her bus. Janice left with her friend Michelle, who always drove her around before school and never offered me a ride even though their school is right behind mine. I took out the last pork chops to defrost so I could Shake 'n Bake them for supper. I never poisoned us even though Janice said it was only a matter of time.

I went to get the new wooden knob I made for the silverware drawer. I wasn't supposed to touch the lathe without an adult standing there, but Annabelle drowned before she could finish teaching me and Mim never had time. So I was real careful. I put on short sleeves and wore the mask and tied my hair back and everything.

Trustworthy—that used to be the main thing about me.

But the knob was all wonky and didn't fit. I took it off and threw it in the woodstove and my eyes ached like I was a person who cried. Then, like every morning since Annabelle died, I went to her room off the kitchen to breathe in the lavender and look at her socks.

Socks were Annabelle's trademark, along with saying

"jeez'm," which not that many people do anymore except me and her. She wore socks with sandals when she could, and they had rainbows and ice-cream cones and stars and things. I gave her the rainbows.

She had forty-seven different pairs and she organized them by color, so I knew there was one pair missing in the purple section and another in the green section. Drove me nuts wondering which was just missing and which was the one she wore the day she died.

One cup olive oil, a quarter cup white vinegar, Annabelle whispered. Made me jump because she didn't usually talk to me in the daytime. *Keeps wood furniture clean and shiny.*

Also, that sister of yours deserves to be horsewhipped.

"Jeez'm, Annabelle." I never heard her say such a thing in my whole life. "I'm losing it," I muttered, slamming the sock drawer shut and booking it out of the room.

All of a sudden it was late. I grabbed an elastic so my best friend Rachel could French braid my hair in homeroom, squeezed my feet into my stupid, too-tight shoes, and hustled for the hillside steps behind our house. They went up to Mrs. Wittingham's and we used them as a shortcut all the time.

At the top, this little bird barreled out from under Mrs. Wittingham's pricker bushes and ran at me, cheeping like it had something important to say. When I went to step around it, it blocked my path, head cocked sideways so it could look me in the eye.

Annabelle wrote about birds in the Guide, but I never saw one like this: brown and white like a sparrow, but with the beak all wrong and a brown sort of Elvis-y hairdo.

"Look, little guy, I gotta go to school. I'm late." I faked to the left and ran to the right. It chased me a few steps, and I was so busy escaping I forgot the sidewalk upheaval in front of the house and fell splat and scraped my knee and got blood on my good tan shorts. Man, that stung.

Somebody behind the front windows coughed out a laugh—the new lady, I thought, even though the curtains were closed, so I don't know how she saw. There was an old beater station wagon in the driveway.

I sat on the sidewalk a minute, spitting on my finger and rubbing the scrape. Usually Rachel would be waiting for me but it was probably too late.

Weirdly, the little bird hunkered down in the middle of the path next to me. What a bizarro bird. *Always feed the birds*, Annabelle whispered. *And wash bloodstains in cold water.*

A spicy, swampy smell hung in the air like nothing I ever smelled before—sort of musty, almost pleasant, but not really.

Why only almost pleasant? the Annabelle voice whispered. *I think it's lovely.*

Except Annabelle hated weird smells.

"Annabelle," I said. "You are starting to freak me out."

Ah. My apologies. I'll do better.

I waited a minute, rubbing my knee, but she never said another word.

"You okay?" said a voice behind me.

CHAPTER TWO

The Ley Line

I looked up from my bloody knee and it was Hippie Hillyard, this kid from my class who wore a ponytail and a leather vest and scarves around his neck in all kinds of colors. Most everybody else wore shirts and jeans, and they were mostly scarf-free.

Hillyard's mom homeschooled him up to last fall. About the third thing he said to us was TV rots your brain. In class, he was the one quiet kid in the room when everybody else was bouncing all over the place.

Hillyard's mom is a biologist, and during our ecology unit he showed us how to measure the mercury and other bad stuff in our river. We can't even eat the fish anymore, at least not very often.

Hillyard said everybody should care about the river. He said we're all made of water and the river's like a relative. One time I told him the river drowned Annabelle. He said no, the river doesn't drown people, it just does what it does and we do what we do and sometimes we get in each other's way. Interesting, I guess, but I didn't feel like talking to him for a while after.

That was Hillyard for you. He made our ecology unit way more fun than anybody expected, but he still went around saying our brains were rotting so he didn't get any more popular.

If Annabelle was alive I would've had to be nice to him *because* he had no friends, but after she died the kindness pretty much drained out of me.

Anyways. Why Hillyard was on Upper Street Monday morning, I had no idea. I thought he lived on some farm someplace.

"I'm fine," I said. My backpack was all spilled on the ground, including Florinda, the My Little Pony Annabelle gave me when I was eight. I kept her in a special pocket in my backpack because . . . I dunno. She was grimy. She had wings.

I grabbed her and stuck her in her pocket before Hillyard could see.

You'd think a person would keep walking and let another person get up and put her backpack on in peace, but no, he stood there waiting. When I got going, he walked with me, even though in my class girls and boys did not normally walk together, plus he was Hippie Hillyard.

Usually I stop at this one place where you can see the river between the houses and, you know, say goodbye for the day, but I wasn't about to do that with somebody I hardly knew.

So it was weird when he stopped instead. "You can get a last look at the river from here," he said. "You probably didn't know that."

I didn't say anything.

Sweet boy, Annabelle whispered. *Be kind to him.*

If you wanted me to be kind to Hippie Hillyard, I thought, you shouldn't have died.

My dear child. Is this what you've been feeling all this time? How horrible.

It was pretty horrible, I had to admit.

We started walking again.

"You must be wondering why I wasn't in school Friday," Hillyard said. (Which I wasn't.) "We moved into the house on the corner."

"The Grays' house?" I saw the moving van but I didn't know it was hippies.

"Yup. My dad's going to use the shed for a workshop. He's starting his own carpentry business."

Now I was the one who stopped walking. For months, I was waiting for Mim to start Annabelle's carpentry business all by herself and make a ton of money so I didn't have to go to Cousin Betty's. And now there'd be a carpenter in the neighborhood already.

We might as well sell every one of those tools. I might as well start packing. Annabelle was deader than ever.

Hillyard realized I wasn't moving. "What's up?"

"Nothing."

I hope his father hits his thumb with a hammer, Annabelle whispered. Definitely not a Guide to Everyday Household Mechanics comment—not much of an Annabelle comment at all, which was bizarre.

On the other hand, someone who loved me was riding around in my head. Better than a stick in the eye, you know?

All the way to Dave Pelletier's used car lot on the corner, Hillyard talked. He said his dad started other businesses in the past but this one was going to work and he was going to paint his room with leftover paint and it was going to be five colors, all swirly on the ceiling.

"That'll be fine till you get the flu," I said. "Then it'll make you puke."

I didn't see Mr. Pelletier anywhere and the car lot looked closed. Strange, because Mr. Pelletier was *always* there, with his Elvis hair and beige suit, waving his hands around so some poor person wouldn't notice what a bad car he was selling them.

All the way up School Street Hillyard talked about how he didn't eat meat and how the pasta always stuck together at hot lunch. Tater Tots were his favorite.

He stayed with me the whole way to my locker like we were besties. None of the other kids said anything, which was good because I never know what to say when somebody says something.

As I unloaded my backpack in my locker, I realized something terrible: If Hippie Hillyard figured he could be friends with me, I was even less popular than I thought.

I used to do okay as far as popularity. When Annabelle drowned right before school started, she was front-page news and everyone was real, real nice to me. But that wore off and something else changed. Stuff that used to be so interesting—the best online video, who could draw the ugliest zombie, how mean Amelda was on *Witchery Girl*—seemed stupid compared to real life. I wasn't up on *Witchery Girl* anyways because we stopped cable and didn't have Netflix or Hulu or anything. All I had to talk about was Shake 'n Bake pork chops or the many household uses for baking soda—even to Rachel. I tried to be normal, I swear, but finally I quit trying.

Rachel was at her locker—last fall we made sure we were next to each other, like we've been since kindergarten. She was acting funny, not looking at me. All I could see was brown hair and a green barrette and one cheek that was blotchy red and white, like she was blushing. On the other side of her, Taylor and Mei Xing were laughing so hard they fell into their lockers.

"Rachel," Taylor gasped, "remember this? Rachel. Look at me."

I could tell Rachel didn't want to look for some reason, but she did and Taylor crossed her eyes and made these snorting noises and grunted something—"pig-breath," probably a line from some movie. She and Mei Xing cracked up big-time. Rachel's cheek got redder and she shot me a side glance.

"What's going on?" I asked. Rachel and Mei Xing and Taylor and Sarah were forty-four percent of the girls' basketball B-team, so they hung out together a lot.

"Nothing," Rachel said.

"Hey, Taylor," yelled Jillie, who's not even in our class, for Pete's sake. "I slept all afternoon yesterday and I still went to bed right after supper." Then she grunted "pig-breath" like Taylor did.

And I knew. I looked at Rachel. She finally looked back at me.

"So . . ." I said. "There was a sleepover?"

She looked like she swallowed a lump of squash. "Taylor texted last minute. I didn't know you weren't invited. Not till I got there."

Of course it had to be Taylor. She showed up in our class four years ago—she's from away, meaning someplace other than Maine—and she tried to be Rachel's best friend, except that was already me. In the beginning she said I had big ears and was a math nerd, but Rachel didn't like that so she stopped. Now she said sneaky stuff like, "Donna, how come I don't have you in my contacts?" when she knew I didn't have a cell phone. She did that three times in, like, six months.

Our school has quite a few people from away. Their parents work up to the university, same as Mim. Annabelle used to say our ancestors were from away even if we were born here—except Sarah's because she and her mom are Mi'kmaq, which is pretty much the opposite of "from away."

I wished Taylor wasn't so good at sports and eye makeup. She taught Rachel how to do a smoky eye, which I didn't even know there was such a thing. And now Rachel was on the B-team and I wasn't, because I can't dribble the ball without tripping over it. And I couldn't afford going to movies or anything, so sometimes we went a whole weekend without seeing each other.

If Rachel was still my best friend she would've called me up before the sleepover to find out what I was bringing for snacks. She could've used the landline. We still had that.

"I'm pretty sure Taylor forgot about you," she said, like that made it better. "Because she couldn't, you know . . ." She got redder.

"Text me. Right." I marched into homeroom like I didn't care, and about ran for the back row of desks so nobody would notice if I lost it a little. I didn't save a seat for Rachel so she could French braid my hair, which hung down like dead seaweed. Rachel sat with Mei Xing and did her hair instead, even though it's only shoulder-length. I was mad at Rachel, maybe. I swallowed it down.

No, no, Annabelle whispered. *The thing to do with anger is blow it out your nose and hope it hits somebody.*

Huh?

As a pick-me-up, make a tea of peppermint and rosemary.

This was getting way too peculiar. I couldn't remember Annabelle ever blowing anger out her nose.

Backing away now, Annabelle whispered.

At lunchtime, to prove nobody hurt my feelings, I made a point of sitting with Rachel and Mei Xing and even Taylor, who left an empty seat between us, which was cold if you want my opinion. She made her long, thick red hair hang down between us like a curtain.

Hillyard came out of the lunch line and I absolutely did not make eye contact, but he went right for that empty seat between me and Taylor and plunked down his tray real fast, like he wanted to get it over with.

Usually he ate at the hopeless table with Mr. Mansfield the custodian and some other nerdy kids.

Rachel froze, a forkful of mac and cheese halfway to her mouth.

"Good afternoon," Hillyard said. "Although strictly speaking it's still morning."

Rachel put down her fork. "Did we invite you to sit with us?" Rachel says stuff other people only think. She and Taylor actually do have a lot in common.

Hillyard concentrated real hard on opening up his milk container. "Nobody was sitting here."

"This table is all girls," said Sarah, who likes to keep things orderly. She was sitting across from him, next to Rachel. He didn't look at her but his ears went red the way they always do if Sarah talks to him, I guess because she's cute.

I don't know what would've happened next except Taylor blurted out something about some fantasy show with mythical beasts in it, and that got everybody arguing. Magic is this big, huge deal for Taylor, ever since second grade—she has a wand, and she knows, like, seventeen different dragon breeds. The rest of the B-team likes that stuff too except Rachel, who's more into reality. Sarah has this epic Lord of the Rings collection. Mei Xing draws merpeople all the time, probably because her mom's an ocean scientist.

I had no clue what was going on in that show—no cable, remember? Hillyard and I sat there eating our mac and cheese like we were at the hopeless table. Even Rachel usually watched the show, but she wasn't up on that week's episode either—her parents were in Australia and her aunt Dana wouldn't let her watch TV on school nights. She knew the characters, though, so at least she could fake it.

"No, no, NO!" Mei Xing yelled, cutting everybody else off. "It's because they call up earth energy when they get mad."

Hillyard brightened up. "My uncle Patrick says there are these lines of energy all over the world, like a grid, and one line runs right through this town and it gives people mystical powers."

Taylor rolled her eyes. "Duh. Everybody knows that. They're called ley lines." She looked at Hillyard anyways, like he might have something interesting to say for the second time in the whole year.

"Actually, my dad says Uncle Patrick's an idiot," Hillyard said. "Dad says ley lines are made up." He thought about what to say next. "Uncle Patrick believes in ghosts. And pixies."

"We all believe in pixies," Taylor said. "They flit past the corner of your eye and when you look they're not there."

"Don't you think that's sorta convenient?" Hillyard said. "That they're not there when you look?"

"The house next door to me has ghosts or something," Sarah said, and of course Hillyard went all red again because she was looking at him with, like, her eyes. "It's empty again because people keep moving out. It's mystical energy from the ley line doing weird stuff, my dad says."

"I bet Hillyard's dad thinks your dad's an idiot." Taylor picked up her tray. "I bet Hillyard thinks we're all idiots. I'm going outside. Coming, Rachel?"

Hillyard opened up his mouth like he was going to say *No, I don't think you're idiots* but instead he said, "You didn't eat your green beans."

Taylor blew air out her mouth and stomped off to the dish room. The others followed.

Hillyard watched them go, slumped in his chair. "I promised my mom I'd try harder."

I got up too. "Maybe you shouldn't bother." I swore to myself Hippie Hillyard was not dragging me down to his level. After I dropped off my tray he was still at the table, using his fork to make designs on his plate with leftover cheese. *No act of kindness, however small, is ever wasted,* Annabelle murmured. That's from the Guide. Actually it's from Aesop, some Greek guy. What did he know.

I went outside so I could hang around like a loser watching Rachel and Taylor shoot baskets.

After school, I made it out the door without Hillyard.

I had exactly fifteen dollars from Mim to spend at Johnson's Food Mart—enough to get eggs, bread, three bags of the kind of frozen corn Annabelle said they should feed to cattle, maybe peanut butter and cheese. I went by the cookie aisle and inhaled. We had dollar-store brownie mix at home but we were saving it for a special occasion.

I went to cash out with Rachel's aunt Dana, who was tending the store while Rachel's parents were away. She beamed at me because I guess she didn't know about my sleepover shame.

The checkout system wasn't working right—Aunt Dana swiped the guy's stuff ahead of me and the register said it cost, like, five hundred dollars. "Cussid ley line," she said, like she was joking, and the guy laughed, and she switched to the manual register.

"Rachel's not here yet," she said when my turn came. Rachel bags after school. "Kid gets later every day. You're all so *busy*." She yammered on, punching my stuff in, but I wasn't listening, watching the register.

When she was done, it said sixteen dollars and thirty-four cents.

I grabbed one bag of corn. "I'll take this back." The

guy behind me in line groaned and Dana glared at him like he was a worm in some broccoli.

"Don't take it back, dear," she said, but I was already elbowing past the guy and booking it for the frozen food section. I didn't look anybody in the eye when I got back and Dana just took my money because I guess she thought I was going to cry if she was nice to me.

At home, I was putting the pork chops in the oven when Mim came in with a bag of groceries.

"Uh, I went shopping too," I said. "I spent the fifteen dollars."

She dropped her bag on the table. "I didn't have the cash with me, so I used credit." She rubbed her forehead like it hurt. "I got corn and eggs and peanut butter and bread."

"Me too. Plus cheese."

She nodded in a tired way, and slung a bag of corn in the freezer. "I'll go by tomorrow and see if they'll take my stuff back."

The only thing Mim hates worse than having no money is somebody knowing about it.

She slumped into a chair and looked out at the shop building under the maple tree.

"Um," I said. "The Grays' house on the corner . . ."

"Yeah. I heard, Girlie-cue. New carpentry business."

She stood up and went for the living room door. "Changing my clothes." And she was gone.

I was doing my math homework and I let supper cook too long, so the pork chops were tough and the frozen fries were dark and crunchy and the frozen corn was mush. I felt like a big failure in the taking-over-for-Annabelle department.

Janice refused to eat the fries because they made her tongue stud hurt, so Mim erupted like Krakatoa the volcano about how stupid it was to get your tongue pierced. Janice stomped upstairs to her room without even putting her plate in the sink.

Before Annabelle died, there was a glass paperweight on the table and you held it when it was your turn to talk about your day. The paperweight was over on the windowsill now, next to the easy chair where Annabelle used to knit.

Why is Janice so unpleasant?

"She wasn't always like this, you know," I said without thinking.

Mim looked up from her mushy corn, which she was pushing around with her fork. "I do know."

I was afraid I made her feel bad. "I mean, things are sort of different." Understatement of the century.

Mim didn't say anything, just scraped her corn into the compost bin and put her plate in the sink. She sat down at her laptop to do data entry for an insurance company, which she started doing over the winter, which is why we still have internet.

I loaded the dishwasher and went back to my homework.

My room's off the kitchen, next to the downstairs bathroom, which is next to Annabelle's room, which is next to the TV room—all added on when Mim and Annabelle did the big renovation.

Before the addition, Janice and I shared a room upstairs, but it's all hers now. When I was real little and she was in third or fourth grade, we'd get in her bed and she'd read to me and sometimes we fell asleep there, and in the morning I'd whisper, "Are you awake?" and she'd say, "Let's get cereal."

I moved downstairs when I was six, so Annabelle wouldn't be alone down here. Janice snuck down every night for a week to crawl in bed with me till I got used to being by myself.

My room, I gotta say, is amazing. The closet door has Annabelle's carving of *The Wild Swans*, this fairy tale she used to read to me. On the windowsill by my bed, she carved a dancing mouse with a hat and a cane. I see him first thing in the morning. His name is Herbert.

That night, I sneaked ahead in my math workbook to cheer myself up, blew off language arts, and went to bed. Florinda was under my pillow, the Big Dipper glowing on my ceiling overhead. Like always, I traced Herbert's outline with my finger before I closed my eyes.

Around midnight, something woke me up. Couldn't get back to sleep. Annabelle tried to relax me by talking about pouring baking soda, salt, and vinegar down a clogged sink, even though knowing that kind of information was exactly why I didn't have friends anymore.

It's very satisfying unclogging a sink. I don't understand why nobody understands that.

Those children at school should be fish bait, Annabelle whispered.

"Jeez'm, Annabelle. That's harsh."

A door slammed someplace, maybe at Mrs. Wittingham's. *Ahhh,* Annabelle murmured. *I have to go now.*

There was this *whump, whump* noise, faint at first but pretty soon it was like a thousand eagles flying over your head.

Joy, Annabelle whispered, which made no sense.

I got up on my knees and threw open the window over my bed. That spicy, swampy smell wafted in at me. "Hello?" I called, though why I thought a thousand eagles would talk to me I can't tell you. Anyways, they didn't. "Okay," I whispered. "All right. Okay."

As I lay down again, Annabelle said, *Hearing things, Petunia. Go to sleep.*

Annabelle did call me Petunia sometimes.

CHAPTER THREE

A Spiky Whale. Obviously.

The week did not improve, at least not for my family.
On Wednesday, Rachel told me her aunt Dana refused to let Mim bring back the groceries and forced her to take them for free.

On Thursday, Mim got a bill from the credit union that made her tighten up her lips.

Friday afternoon, she noticed my toes sticking out too far in front of my sandals and made Janice take me to Goodwill, where we got some butt-ugly, super-floppy sandals and way-too-big sneakers.

Janice played with her tongue stud *all* week, and there was a lot of door slamming. I went to bed earlier and earlier so I could listen to Annabelle talk me to sleep.

Looking for fun when cleaning the toilet? Pour in a

packet of orange Kool-Aid. It really works! Also, your
sister is supremely annoying.

Okay, that last thing could've been me. Except, who says "supremely"?

We never caught sight of the new lady at Mrs. Wittingham's and we cut through her yard all the time, so it was embarrassing that we were strangers.

Saturday morning, I decided we had to do the welcome-to-the-neighborhood thing the way Annabelle used to, which meant using up our brownie mix.

Mim came in with her laptop and sniffed the air. "Mmm."

"For the new neighbor. Annabelle always—"

"I remember."

I was on my hands and knees taking out the dishwasher filter so I could clean it, with Annabelle's Guide beside me.

"Sure you know what you're doing there, Girlie-cue?"

Jeez'm, anybody can do a dishwasher filter. In fact, that's exactly what it says in the Guide: *Anybody can do this. Calm down.* I dumped the filter parts in the sink so I could wash them.

Janice came in because she smelled chocolate. We decided we each could have one brownie and take the rest to the new lady. Mim said Janice and I could split hers. For five seconds we were warm and normal.

But then Janice clicked her tongue stud on her teeth, and I guess Mim remembered Janice got home late the night before smelling all smoky with beer on her breath. So she said, "Actually, Donna, you can have all of mine. *And* Janice's."

Vilma Bliksem turned out to be about a million years old, six feet tall and skinny, wearing leather pants and a wool vest and this soft blue shirt buttoned up to her neck, plus black knee-high boots with red laces. Her gray hair was pulled back in a bun and she had bushy eyebrows and this long, straight nose.

When she opened her door and we were standing there with our plate of brownies, her mouth cranked into a smile that looked like somebody jabbed her in the gut with a sharp pencil.

Mim held out the brownies. "Welcome to the neighborhood. We're the Landons from down below. I'm Nan. My daughters are Janice and Donna." Mim's real name is Nancy Jane, but she hates it.

The pencil-jab smile wobbled. "I am Vilma Bliksem." She had a little accent. "I do not eat sweets."

"You from away?" Janice asked.

"Janice!" Mim said, because I guess that was rude.

"Not your business," Vilma Bliksem said.

She didn't take the brownies. Mim pulled the plate

back to her chest. "We just wanted . . . we wanted . . ."
Mim doesn't do social stuff that well. That was all Annabelle.

Vilma Bliksem cranked up her smile and stepped back from the doorway. "Please. Come inside."

Inside was dim with a faint haze of stink—raccoons got into Mrs. Wittingham's house while it was empty over the winter. Her kids hired professional exterminators, but the house definitely remembered it used to have raccoons.

Mrs. Wittingham's dingy old sofa was right where it always was, also the raggedy recliner and padded rocker. Except now there was a fancy wooden coffee table with what looked like real raccoon feet.

Janice looked close. "Interesting table."

"I am out of practice." Ms. Bliksem turned her head and gave me this piercing look, right in the eyes. "It is good to work with your hands."

"I work with my hands," I said.

"I know."

"How do you know?" Janice asked.

Ms. Bliksem gave her a look like this vocabulary word we had, "baleful," which means a certain kind of angry. Ms. Bliksem looked baleful as heck.

Janice smiled at her, just to be annoying.

"So," Mim said, working hard to save the conversation. "What brings you to our little town?"

"The river. And"—baleful glare—"I followed a line."

I blinked a couple times, decided she meant a latitude line. *How about a ley line?* Annabelle murmured.

I thought about that.

Nah.

"Guess we should go home now," I said.

Mim looked at me like I was the most brilliant thing in the world. "Yep. Another busy Saturday. Heh-heh." She held out the brownie plate. "Want to keep these, 'case you have guests?"

Vilma Bliksem didn't look like much of a hostess, but she reached for the plate. "Yes. Perhaps I will eat some."

Her sleeve hiked up so we could see her wrist, which had a squiggly green-and-red tattoo. I couldn't see what it was but Janice was closer and she let out a gasp. "Whoa, cool dragon."

Ms. Bliksem pulled her sleeve over the tattoo. "It is nothing. Thank you for the cakes."

"They're called brownies." Janice smiled as if she said something amazing, which is one reason everybody thinks she's so smart. The other reason is that she is.

"Brownies," Ms. Bliksem repeated. "Thank you. Goodbye."

The door slammed behind us and two locks clicked. As we headed for the steps down the hill to our yard, the little bizarro bird rushed out at us from under the pricker bushes, chirping and flapping and trying to slow us down. Tough luck, birdie—we almost ran down the steps.

"Criminal waste of brownie mix," Janice panted.

"That house needs work," Mim said.

"Needs new gutters out front," I said.

"Oh of course," Janice said. "Let's talk about home maintenance. The woman has a *dragon tattoo*, for crying out loud. Her coffee table has raccoon feet!"

We made it to our back deck. "I'm going to punch in some numbers before Harriman's," Mim said. She cleaned and did the books at Harriman's Bakery Saturdays and Sundays. Her *third* job.

"Michelle's picking me up for work," Janice said. The two of them worked weekends at McDonald's up to the mall. She gave Mim half her money to help pay bills. I wanted to get a job—anything to stay away from Cousin Betty and the boys—but I was too young for a work permit and the older kids got all the babysitting jobs.

Mim gave Janice a tired look. "I'm not sure I want you driving with Michelle after last night."

"Oh yeah, Nancy Jane? How else do I get to the mall?" Janice barged past us, then turned to look Mim in the eye. "And I can't tell her not to come because I don't have a *phone*." The screen door slapped shut behind her.

"Be home by six," Mim called after her. "You're grounded tonight."

* * *

Inside, Mim looked at her laptop. "Oh. We missed a chat with Betty." She caught me trying to sneak out the screen door. "We're calling her back, Donna. Stay here."

I plunked my butt on the windowsill by the door and tried to hear the rapids.

Judging from your thoughts, Annabelle said, *this Cousin Betty seems . . . unsavory.* Which was a funny way to put it, considering Annabelle used to *live* with her. Mim opened up her chat program and two minutes later I heard Cousin Betty's raspy voice.

"Sorry we missed you," Mim said. "We were taking brownies to a new neighbor."

"Ooo, brownies," Betty said. "Guess the finances are looking up, hey, Nancy Jane? No more cornflake suppers for you!"

Mim stiffened. "We never had cornflakes for supper and we never will."

"I'm teasing you, dearie. Where's my little Donna?"

"She's right here." Mim gave me a look I couldn't ignore, so I hunched myself in next to her where Cousin Betty could see me. And there she was: sharp-chinned face, blaze-orange hair.

I couldn't wait to tell Janice Cousin Betty was using her same hair color.

"Look at you, dearie," Cousin Betty said. "Ain't you cunnin'?"

"Not really."

Mim gave me an elbow. "She's growing up fast."

"I can see that. That T-shirt's a little on the small side, isn't it?"

"It's fine." I tried to stretch my shirt over the belt of my shorts but it wouldn't go.

"Well, that pullout couch's waiting for you, whenever you want to visit."

"We haven't decided yet—" Mim started, but Betty rolled right over her.

"Did you ask for a raise like I told you to?" She said it like she was Mim's boss or something.

Mim sat up straighter. "Betty, my salary is none of your—"

Cousin Betty gave an ear-wreck of a screech. "Anthony! Did I see you stick that cat in the fridge?" Anthony was the *nice* twin. "Hang on, Nancy Jane. I gotta deal with this." Betty's face disappeared from the screen. We heard a slap and a kid's wail.

"Mim," I whispered. "I can't go live there."

Her mouth went straight. "Janice and I will be working all summer and you can't stay home alone every day and she's our only relative. It'll be like going away to camp." I noticed she couldn't look at me and say that.

Cousin Betty was back. "Sorry, Nancy Jane. Can't believe how smart that kid is. An oxygen experiment—did you ever hear such a thing from a six-year-old?"

"No," Mim said.

"They must get it from the TV. Well, I gotta go, dear. Let me know when you're sending me my little Donna. I can buy her new clothes. Can't wait to dress up a little girl! Maybe she can stay for the school year, even."

"Betty, we haven't decided—"

"Bye, dear!" The computer made a swooshing sound, and Cousin Betty was gone.

The *school year*? "Mim—"

"I know, Donna. I *know*." Mim squinted at the clock on the laptop. "GAH! It's ten already!" She grabbed her purse. "I don't want you going down to the river by yourself, hear me?" She said that every Saturday since Annabelle died.

After she left I took off my too-big shoes so they wouldn't trip me and headed for Table Rock. I *needed* to be by the river. Mim would never know.

Me and Rachel used to spend whole Saturdays sitting down there with Annabelle and Janice and a couple other kids, splashing our feet and hucking rocks into the water and pretending to fish. Table Rock stuck way out into the river, and our moms never let us jump off the end because of the funny currents, but there was a pool of water on the side where you could dunk yourself and have a splash fight on a hot day.

Janice and me had our feet in that pool the day Annabelle died.

She used to boogie out onto the rock and fling her arms open and holler: "River runs free, river runs free, like a glittering seam of stars!" It was from some poem she copied into the back of the Guide. We all groaned, because she said the same thing every time.

We built pixie houses out of driftwood and junk—Annabelle said if we looked out for the littlest creatures they'd look out for us. Mim came with us sometimes and she taught me to make these amazing teeny little stone houses, all fitted together so they'd last for years. One day she said I had a feel for construction. I think about that day a lot.

I asked Mim one time if pixies would move into the stone houses too. She looked at me like I knocked the wind out of her and she scowled at Annabelle for some reason and said, "Maybe a mouse." Annabelle rolled her eyes.

Mim's sort of a nonfiction person.

Annabelle always made sure there was a little indentation in the rock—sort of a basin—outside each doorway, and she left a metal measuring cup down there so we could fill the basins with water every day or two. She said pixies have to bathe in river water at dawn in order to stay magical, but they're afraid to go in the river at that hour because of the fish.

We left pieces of candy bars in the houses, especially the big one up by the rosebushes because it looked like somebody *had* to live there. I figured mice would like candy just as much as pixies. Annabelle got the candy for me. We didn't tell Mim.

Janice never came to the river anymore. Mim hardly even looked at it.

Beautiful river, Annabelle whispered in my head.

"A glittering seam of stars," I reminded her.

If you say so. And good fish. Which was a strange thing to say. We only ate river fish about once a year, because of the toxic mercury.

I felt bad I didn't have any candy with me, so I figured I could at least fill the water bowls by the houses. They were already full, which was weird because I couldn't remember the last time it rained.

I closed my eyes and took in a deep breath, smelled the freshness of the water, feeling my muscles unknot. No matter what was going on, this river *always* made me feel better. Out at the end of Table Rock, I lay down and the river sang me a lullaby of murmurs and sloshes. I dozed off.

Whuff. Splurt. Whuff.

Odd noise.

That weird spicy, swampy smell was back.

Something snuffled at my bare foot—something with hot breath. I opened my eyes and lay there blinking up at the sky, sort of afraid to look.

Something in the river made an extra-big *sploosh*. I sat up like a jack-in-the-box.

About ten feet from the end of the rock, the water swirled in a circle, like something huge just went under. I gave a closed-mouth shriek and scrambled up on my feet.

Something ginormous was heading downstream towards the city. Something with spikes on its back.

It's a whale, Petunia, whispered Annabelle. *A spiky whale. Nothing to worry about.*

I was pretty sure whales didn't come up the river that far. Too shallow. Annabelle had this friend who was a game warden, Arthur Libby, and I bet he'd know. But I never saw him anymore.

Hillyard always yammered on about the northern pike, this big fish somebody brought to Maine that eats up all the native fish. Maybe they had spikes.

Obviously, Petunia. That must be it.

Obviously.

CHAPTER FOUR

Minimum Wage

I didn't tell anyone what I saw in the river. I was pretty sure I was half-asleep or it was an optical illusion. Just a bunch of extra-big northern pike swimming in a row. *Extra, extra-big northern pike. Absolutely.* Annabelle's voice made it sound like I was a big silly to think there was something huge in the river.

Turned out I wasn't, of course. But at the time, Annabelle's "aren't you silly" tone of voice made me feel bad. She sounded that same way the last night I saw her, except then it was Mim she thought was being silly.

Mim decided to cook that night, even though she *never* cooked—Annabelle always did, and I guess she was insulted, because she started acting all weird. She kept bugging Mim while she tried to brown the pork chops, giving her advice, calling her Nancy Jane.

Finally, Mim slammed her fork down on the counter. "This is how it'll always be, isn't it? You will never, *ever* decide I know how to do *a cussid thing.*"

Annabelle looked at me and I knew I was supposed to be on her side, but I was too confused to say anything. So Annabelle walked into her room and snapped the door shut, and that's when I figured out this wasn't about cooking.

It was about that carpentry business out back with the red truck, waiting for Mim to quit her job. Annabelle was used to being everybody's teacher, even Mim, and that's probably the way it always was, even when they were little. I knew Mim was worried about all the loans they took out, but until then I didn't know she was nervous about working with her big sister.

Later, when I knocked on Annabelle's door, her voice didn't sound just right. So I went in and she was lying on their grammy's quilt, blowing her nose with her eyes all red, and I didn't know what to say except "Supper's ready."

We all made a big deal about how good the pork chops were—they tasted great, even though they were every bit as tough as Annabelle said they'd be. "You're all being very patronizing," Mim said, and she left the table early and Janice went to Michelle's without doing a single dish.

"Jeez'm crow," Annabelle muttered, and I said, "I'll do the dishes."

"We both will," she said. "Finest kind." That's what older people say if something's super good. But I knew I hurt her feelings, not standing up for her and all.

Next morning, Annabelle got up before any of us and went off kayaking with her friend Carol before I even brushed my teeth.

She never came back.

I wondered if she thought we didn't love her.

Rachel came over the minute she heard and she cried like anything. I wanted to but I couldn't—it was like this big ball of tears settled in my chest and turned into a rock.

I never cried all winter. I don't think Mim or Janice did either.

Now, as I rolled over and punched my pillow, wishing I could sleep, the voice in my head said, *It's all right, Petunia. I knew I was loved.*

I so, so wanted that voice to be Annabelle.

Monday morning was when something very amazing happened.

First thing, late as usual, I skittered up the hillside steps to find Bizarro Bird huddled by Vilma Bliksem's pricker bushes, looking raggedy and moldy.

The back door slammed open, and Ms. Bliksem stuck her head out. The bird squawked and booked it under this old shed on cement blocks at the top of the steps. "Good morning, Ms. Bliksem," I said, extra, extra polite. "I hope you don't mind . . . We always use the steps . . ."

She waved her hand in the air. "It's okay." She stood there with the door open. She gave me her pencil-jab smile.

"I have to get to school," I said.

"Yes, yes. But first . . ." She stood there. I stood there. Our lives ticked by.

"This house is very dirty."

"Oh." No kidding.

"It is too much. I need help to clean. Will you find someone? Your sister or your mother? I will pay."

"*I'll* do it," I said. Just the job I needed.

Her smile faded. "No. You are too young."

"I clean all the time. Really."

Ms. Bliksem chewed her lip. "Start now."

"I have to go to school."

Ms. Bliksem scowled.

Careful, Petunia, Annabelle whispered. So I added in a rush, "I'll be back at quarter of four. I promise."

She gave a sharp nod and went back inside.

Interesting, Annabelle murmured.

I almost danced to school, making plans. I'd go home first and get dinner started, come back and clean a couple hours, go eat, do homework. If I made enough money, there'd be no more Cousin Betty and her Evil Boy Twins.

Finest kind.

I was way late for school (no sign of Rachel *or* Hillyard), so I got recess detention. But art class was almost good. We were making papier-mâché marionettes and my guy's mustache dripped all over his chin. But he could walk and wave and his wrists moved in four directions because I stole a couple plastic universal joints from Mim and Annabelle's shop.

"Too bad about the mustache," Mr. Corcoran said. "How'd you do that with the wrists?"

I showed everybody, and for a minute or two I was a celebrity but then I went into too much detail about the many interesting features of universal joints and everybody went back to their own marionettes.

That teacher. He collects troll dolls.

Huh? "How do you know that?" I whispered.

Never you mind.

She had insights from the Great Beyond, I figured.

I had nothing to do now and I couldn't help looking at Hillyard's marionette, which he was working on all by himself in a corner like always. It was this amazing bird with individual feathers he painted in about thirty-seven colors. I couldn't believe something like that came out of a person's head.

Hillyard made his wings in three parts so they could flap but they weren't moving right and the strings he glued to them kept ripping off. But I kept looking, and I pretty much had it figured out when Hillyard carefully put the bird down and pounded the table with his fists.

The good thing about not being Ms. Popularity is nobody notices when you walk over to the hippie kid's corner and say "I think I know what to do with those wings."

He looked at me kinda bleary-eyed. "You gotta bore holes," I said, "and thread fishing line through and make cloth hinges."

Hillyard looked at his bird. "Huh," he said.

I pulled up a stool. He went to the fabric bin and came back with supplies.

We glued the hinges on, bored holes, and strung fishing line, but it turned out the line cut into the papier-mâché and sliced one wing so bad it almost fell apart.

"Oh, man," I said. "This is bad." Hillyard didn't freak out, though, only chewed his lip and narrowed his eyes.

"We need a buffer," he said.

"Amazing." I saw what he meant: You'd glue the canvas in the holes and anyplace else you needed to protect the papier-mâché.

"How'd you think up all these colors?" I said while we glued.

He shrugged. "I have a color wheel on my wall at home."

We were having such a good time we didn't even hear the bell ring for recess. Mr. Corcoran let us keep on working right up till social studies, said I could do my tardiness detention right there. The bird was almost done and you could see it was going to flap like anything.

It was the best time I had with another person since Annabelle died.

But then me and Hillyard walked into social studies and Taylor, she went, "Woo-WOOoo, Donna, did you kiss him?" in front of the whole class. Rachel laughed, my face got hot, everybody else went, "Woo-WOOoo," and it was obvious I didn't have a friend in the world.

In math class I felt Rachel and Taylor staring at me from the two back corners. We made an isosceles triangle.

Your friend, that Rachel. She feels guilty about mocking you.

"So why'd she do it?" I whispered into my fractions workbook.

I don't understand it either, to be honest.

By the time the last bell rang, I was actually looking forward to cleaning Ms. Bliksem's house.

At home I glopped together the mushroom soup

chicken bake from Annabelle's Guide, stuck it in the oven, and set it to turn on later. I grabbed the Guide and cleaning stuff and huffed and puffed up the steps to Vilma Bliksem's.

When she let me in, it was all I could do not to run away and puke. Raccoon stink was everywhere.

"You should open the windows," I said.

"People will see in."

I looked around the kitchen. "What would they see?"

Somewhere in her throat, a growl started.

Careful, Petunia. I stepped backwards. "S-so, where do you want me to start?"

"Start here." She pointed at the streaky floor. "I tried to wash this. With water, but it made more mess."

Man, that floor was gross. "I can't believe they didn't clean up more of the raccoon stuff before you moved in."

"They said they would do so if I waited a week. I said no, I needed to be under cover now."

"Under cover" seemed like a funny way to put it.

Nothing gets your mind off your troubles like scrubbing raccoon . . . well, whatever . . . off linoleum. As I worked, I wondered why anybody would figure you could wash that floor with just water. Maybe she traveled a lot and lived in hotels. Maybe she was really, really rich and had servants.

What was such a person doing in a raccoon-filthy house in a teeny little Maine town? Our population was, like, a thousand, for Pete's sake.

When my two hours were up, I wandered down the hall and found Ms. Bliksem in the second bedroom, flipping through a little leather book with black hand-writing inside. She snapped it shut fast when I walked in. The low growl started again.

Easy, Petunia.

I put my hands in the air like I was in a stickup.

"Who said you could come in here?" Ms. Bliksem snarled.

"I-I have to go home now. I can come back tomorrow. You owe me money." No way I was coming back unless I knew I'd get paid.

She did an eye-closing, I'm-about-to-lose-it thing. "Who said I would pay you today?"

Ca-a-a-areful.

"I need the money now, and I'm only asking min-imum wage. Anybody else would charge twice that. Probably more."

She marched into the kitchen, which looked a mil-lion times better. She stood there, stunned, then nodded. "Wait here." She went off and returned with a closed fist. "Take this. I have no other currency."

I held out my hand. Nothing happened—she stood

there with her fist hovering over mine. At last she took a deep breath and dropped something on my palm, her hand trembling.

A tiny gold coin.

In my head, Annabelle moaned softly.

Guess Ms. Bliksem really liked that coin, because she folded her arms tight, like she was stopping herself from grabbing it back. It was smaller than a dime, thin and ridiculously bright in my grimy hand. It had some guy's head on it—sort of awkward, like a kid's drawing—and faded words I couldn't read.

"Bite it," she said.

"Huh?"

"If it dents, it is real gold. You must always determine this."

"Real *gold*?" Okay, it *was* soft to the teeth.

I couldn't stop looking at it, poking it, moving it around on my hand.

"Beautiful, yes?" Her voice was so quiet I looked up. She was smiling, a real smile this time.

I nodded and poked it some more. It was so shiny, so pure.

"Be careful," Ms. Bliksem said in the same quiet voice. "The desire for gold can be a sickness." She folded my fingers over so I couldn't see the coin anymore, squeezed my hand so hard it hurt. "Tell no one I have this gold. No one."

She let go, and I put my hand in my pocket, keeping a fist in case there was a hole.

Ms. Bliksem tilted her head at me, not smiling. "You are a child still. You have not yet learned to betray."

What do you say to that? I nodded.

"Gold will never betray you. It is forever. Not like—" She stooped to peer into my eyes. "Not like . . . people."

I thought about Rachel and the sleepover, Janice calling me a sad little person. Annabelle dying. I tightened my fist around my gold piece.

"You understand," Ms. Bliksem whispered, her blue eyes boring into mine.

"Yes," I whispered back.

"Good." She straightened, tugged her vest down over the waistband of her leather pants. "Now. I must"—she swallowed hard—"I must sell some of my gold for your currency. You know where I can do that?"

I shook my head. "I'll ask my mother."

Her eyebrows jutted out, scary as heck.

"I won't tell her you have a *lot* of gold," I said hastily. "Just a little. We can buy mops and things too."

Pencil-jab smile. "Tomorrow. Same time as today. Do not be late."

CHAPTER FIVE

Speed-Walking Freaks

When I got home, weighed down with cleaning stuff, Mim was pouring frozen cow corn into a pot to go with my mushroom chicken. "Where you been? You're a mess."

"I was working for Ms. Bliksem. She's paying me. I'm going after school for two hours every day this week plus more on the weekend, and I'll see if I can keep doing it for a while. Maybe I can fix a few things over there too. I'll make a ton of money. So we can get more groceries and things."

Mim jerked her head back like I hit her. "It's not your job to worry about groceries, Donna."

"I'm not *worried*. I just . . . I don't want to go to Cousin Betty's."

"Girlie-cue." Her eyes went all droopy and sad. "It's going to take more than you getting a part-time job."

"But—"

"Pwobwy 'on't pay you." Janice walked in, fiddling with her tongue stud.

"Shows how much you know." I held out my hand, gold coin shining.

Mim and Janice practically knocked their heads together swooping in to see.

"Who's this guy?" Janice snatched the coin and squinted at the head on it. "What do the words say?"

"Dunno." I grabbed the coin back, because it was mine. "But I'm going with Ms. Bliksem tomorrow to turn it into real money. She has more gold coins . . . just, you know, a few. She needs to cash them in."

"I'm not sure I should let you gallivant around with this woman until I know more about her," Mim said. "I mean, gold coins . . ." She looked over at Annabelle's knitting chair the way she did when she wished her big sister was around to talk things over.

"Don't forget the dragon tattoo," Janice said. "And the raccoon furniture." She leaned over to examine our dinner. "What's this all over the chicken, snot?"

"It's only for a week or two," I said. "And yeah, Janice, I saved up all my snot so I could put it on the chicken and feed it to you."

"Set the table," Mim said to Janice. "And stop fooling with that tongue stud."

Next morning, Mim announced Janice had to go with me to the gold buyer. She thought two of us would be safer than one. She googled up two guys in Bangor who bought and sold precious metals, and got directions to the closest one.

She said I had to pay Janice half my time. "That's no fair," I said, but she was packing her briefcase so she wasn't listening anymore.

Janice stuck out her studded tongue at me. Real mature.

When somebody with a dragon on her wrist pays you in gold coins, you have to tell a friend, no matter what you promised. Better make up with Rachel, I decided, and forget the whole "woo-WOOoo" thing.

I left early to make sure I'd be at Ms. Bliksem's when Rachel went by. Also, that way I'd miss Hillyard, who always seemed to be late. No more "woo-WOOoo" for me. I put a purple elastic in my pocket for when Rachel braided my hair.

Bizarro Bird was looking terrible. He wasn't even hiding, just sat next to the path looking all scrawny. "Hang in there, bird," I said as I passed. "I swear I'll bring food this afternoon." He gave me a tired squawk.

When I saw Rachel coming along Upper Street on the opposite side, I was actually nervous. I waved.

And she waved!

But then, uh-oh. There was Hillyard, coming up on my side of Upper Street in a purple-and-pink tie-dyed T-shirt, leather vest, and battered leather shoes laced on the side. His scarf was yellow and orange stripes. Plus the ponytail, except today he also had a skinny little braid with electric-blue beads hanging down by one ear.

He got to me first. "Hey." And of course he stopped, because I have the worst luck in the universe. Rachel was going to think I *planned* to meet him.

"Hey." I dropped my pack on the sidewalk and made a big deal out of rummaging and rearranging things. "Uh, you go ahead. I gotta do this."

"I'm in no rush. I came early."

I straightened up. "No, seriously. I'm waiting for someone."

Rachel was right across the street, cocking her head exactly twenty degrees, like she does when she's wondering what the heck.

I had to make a break for it. "Hey, Rachel, I'm coming!" I yelled, scooping up my pack and starting across the street. Hillyard made a noise, sort of a groan.

What was it he said at lunch? *I promised my mom I'd try harder.*

Aw, Annabelle whispered.

I felt like mean Amelda on *Witchery Girl.* I turned around in the middle of the street. "Okay. C'mon, Hillyard."

Rachel looked like a stuffed deer head.

"Let's go," I said when Hillyard and I got to her. "We're gonna be late." She marched forward with her shoulders back, walking fast so nobody would think she was with Hippie Hillyard. Rachel's pretty interested in being popular.

Me and Hillyard sped up behind her. We were speed-walking freaks.

"Wonder . . . what's . . . for lunch . . . ." Hillyard was panting. Rachel and I did not reply.

We got to school, did the freak-speed-walk through the playground and into the building. Hillyard happened to be walking next to Rachel when we got to our lockers. He stopped with us and I swear he bowed slightly. "Nice walking with you ladies," he said.

A voice floated down the hall. "Woo-WOOoo. Lookit Rachel and Hillyard!"

Rachel gave a goaty bleat. She shoved her pack into her locker, slammed it shut, and hauled butt for the girls' room. A whole line of boys hooted as she skididdered past them.

Hillyard's ears were bright red. He about ran down the hall to his locker. I went to the girls' room to comfort Rachel, but she was locked in a stall and wouldn't answer me.

What just happened? I'm baffled. Is this typical behavior for you children?

In homeroom, Rachel braided Taylor's hair. She kept saying how amazing and thick it was.

At recess, I stood over by the swings, feeling like everyone was looking at me and also ignoring me.

"Wanna kick the ball around?" And there was Hillyard, a soccer ball in his hands, purple and pink tie-dye gleaming in the sun. Rachel stared at us from second base.

He promised his mom he'd try harder.

"Okay," I said. "All right. Okay."

We went over by the woods where there isn't much grass. We were too far apart to talk much more than "oops, sorry" and "good one." When the bell rang, we walked back to the building together, still silent. But three feet inside the gym door Hillyard said, "I'm trying not to talk so I don't sound like a ninnyhammer." It was about the third-saddest thing I ever heard anybody say. Also, who says "ninnyhammer"?

"You're not a . . . ninnyhammer," I said, lying. "You just know weird stuff."

Hillyard went to his locker and I went to mine. Rachel was there.

"You know Amelda in *Witchery Girl*?" I asked her.

She got out her math book. "Yeah, she's mean." She looked me right in the eye. "I'm not mean and I'm *still*"—she stamped her foot—"not walking to school with that kid." She never stamped at me before. "He's your new best friend, I guess."

"He is *not*." How could she say that? "Anyways, Taylor's yours."

She slammed her locker shut and marched away from me. At the end of the day she left with Taylor and took the long way home, so we weren't on the same street.

All the way down School Street and around the Upper Street corner, Hillyard explained about how the human eye distinguishes color. Something about different lengths of light waves bouncing off your retina.

It was pretty interesting, but not enough to hide one true thing:

Rachel was not my friend anymore.

CHAPTER SIX

Dealer in Precious Metals

Janice was waiting for me at home, her orange hair slicked behind her ears so she'd look older, though why she bothered I have no idea. She has the same sticky-outy ears I do and you automatically look like a kid with ears like that. Also, she had on a hot-pink cotton sweater and a green skirt so short she could've been a cheerleader.

"Cousin Betty called," she said. "Wanting to know the exact day you're out of school."

"Her hair dye's the same color as yours," I said.

I had crumbled up stale crackers so I could feed them to the molting Bizarro Bird. The little guy threw himself at them and chowed down like he was starving.

"Why are you feeding that ugly little bird?" Janice said.

"He needs it. Look at him. It's like he hasn't eaten in days."

Janice put on her Fascinating Facts from High School voice. "If a bird can't feed itself, there's something wrong. You should let nature take its course."

"If you're such a nature nerd, why's your hair that color?"

"You are *so* sad."

Vilma Bliksem was waiting by her car, wearing her leather pants and wool vest but with a green shirt this time and a leather satchel hanging from a strap across her chest. "Who does she think she is, Han Solo?" Janice whispered.

Ms. Bliksem got all thundery-looking when she saw Janice. "Why two?"

I let Janice take that one.

"We don't allow Donna to ride in cars alone with strangers," Janice said. I thought the "we" part was a little much.

"I will not pay for two." Ms. Bliksem didn't seem insulted, to my relief.

"Of course not," Janice said. "Donna and I will share."

Ms. Bliksem pondered, gave a decisive nod. "Get in. The big one in front, to tell me where to go."

Janice opened the front passenger door, which screeched like a dying animal. "Guh. Dave Pelletier strikes again."

Three minutes later the car still hadn't started. Ms. Bliksem—you know what? I'm going to call her Vilma from now on—kept pumping the gas pedal and you could smell the starter burning up.

"Does it always do this?" Janice asked.

"I don't know," Vilma said, pumping the pedal. "The man drove it here for me. He was a greedy little man, but now he's sorry."

"Why?" I blurted.

"Not your business."

"Try leaving the gas pedal alone and just turning the key." Janice drove Michelle's car tons of times, even when she didn't have her learner's permit.

Vilma scowled at Janice, but she did it. The car started. We lurched out the driveway, ran up on the opposite sidewalk, veered back to run over the *other* sidewalk, then corkscrewed down the street, Vilma clinging to the wheel and yelling what I guess were swears in another language.

"Have you driven before?!" Janice yelled.

"No!" Vilma yelled back. "Easier than it looks." We wheeled around the corner and rocketed past the school. The speedometer hit fifty-five and I decided to stop looking.

Janice had her hands braced against the ceiling. "Slow down!" she shrieked. Vilma ran the red light at the end of the street, careened around the corner onto Main Street. Horns blared, tires screeched, and we sideswiped somebody's mailbox. I looked back to see a blue pickup truck run onto the sidewalk.

"Pull over," Janice yelled. "I can drive."

"Quiet," Vilma yelled back. "*I* am driving."

She sure was.

Half an hour later, we wheeled around a corner and lurched to a stop, inches from a brick storefront. A big black sign said "Lukas Altin, Dealer in Precious Metals" in golden letters with swirls and squiggles.

"This must be the place." Janice lowered her hands from the ceiling.

"I like to drive," Vilma said.

A man at a desk in the back stood up as we went in—Mr. Altin, it turned out. He wasn't much taller than Janice, mostly bald, with, like, these ginormous gold cuff links.

Vilma hauled out a burlap bag. It was the size of a three-meatball sub.

Janice's mouth dropped open.

Vilma started to hand the bag to Mr. Altin, then changed her mind and hugged it to her chest like she didn't want to let it go. Her sleeve rode up, exposing the dragon tattoo on her wrist. The gold dealer goggled his eyes at the tattoo and drew back the hand he'd held out for the bag of gold. "What do you want?" he whispered.

"Ah." Vilma tapped her wrist. "You know this sign?"

"I've been a gold dealer for many, many years. I've *seen* that sign."

"Good. You will help me."

"Please." Mr. Altin put his hands together like he was praying. "I do not want this gold."

"It is freely given. It will not harm you."

Would not *harm* him? Janice and I looked at each other. *Don't believe everything you hear,* Annabelle whispered.

"You will take this gold," Vilma said, "and you will tell no one." She hesitated, clinging to the gold, then thrust it away from her and onto Mr. Altin's desk. Her hands were trembling, same as when she gave me my gold piece.

"I-I can't. Please . . ."

Vilma reached into her satchel and pulled out the small leather-bound book I'd seen her leafing through. She gave Mr. Altin a glare that would fry a pancake. "You know what it means to say no to someone like me?"

"Yes, yes. I know very well." He closed his eyes for a second, then reached for the bag of gold. "I-I will accommodate you, madame." His own hands shaking, he weighed a piece of the gold and then the whole sack, jotting down numbers and sighing. Vilma never took her eyes off the gold for a second until he hustled it off into a back room. When that door snapped shut behind him, Vilma shuddered and let out this long, whistling breath.

Then, weirdly, she walked over to a hat rack in the corner, grabbed this fancy tweed cap, and stuck it in her satchel. When she saw we were watching, she glared and said, "I need it." O-o-o-kay.

Mr. Altin returned with a stack of hundred-dollar bills four inches high. Even Vilma looked surprised. "That's very much."

He thrust it at her. "Take it. And please do not come back."

She narrowed her eyes. "I will come back as I please. Be careful, little man." She tucked the stack of bills into her satchel, gestured to me and Janice. "Come."

"Wait." I opened my change purse and took out my coin. "I want to sell this one."

He looked startled at Vilma. "You gave this to a child?"

"I told you, it is freely given. There is no danger."

Mr. Altin shook his head, but held out his hand for my coin. I looked down at it shining in the middle of my palm, so pure, so beautiful. I didn't want to give it to him.

Get rid of that thing, Petunia, Annabelle whispered.

"What's the matter with you?" Janice nudged me with her elbow.

I held out my palm. Mr. Altin snatched the coin and went off to his back room.

My coin was gone.

When he returned, Mr. Altin counted seven twenties into my hand.

"Seriously?" Janice whispered. "Whoa."

"Enough for yesterday and today?" Vilma asked from the doorway.

Okay, now you know what I should've said. I should've told her it was more than twice what she owed me. Janice was watching me, smirking because it must've been obvious what I was thinking.

I kept my back to Vilma. "Uh, yeah. It's fine." My face went hot and my stomach clenched, because Annabelle didn't say anything, but I knew she really hated lies. I made a tube of the twenties and I clutched them tight.

"Bye-bye, Little Miss Reliable," Janice muttered.

Mr. Altin pointed at the door. "Leave me."

We were no sooner out on the sidewalk than the locks clicked behind us and the shade snapped down.

Janice hustled to the driver's-side door.

"*I* will drive," Vilma snarled.

"I know the way to the mop store," Janice said. "But it's hard to describe. Also, you're driving without a license. That's against the law."

Vilma stared at her a minute, then nodded. "This one time." She screeched open the passenger-side door.

"Do you even have your permit with you?" I whispered to Janice.

"You're really going to worry about that now?" Janice waited for Vilma to get her screeching door shut before she started the engine. "While we're at it we better get some de-smellifier for this car."

"That man," Vilma said. "I don't trust him to keep his silence about my gold."

I stuck my twenties in my pocket so I'd forget what a big liar I was.

Vilma muttered to herself all the way to the hardware store.

You should've seen Mim's face when we gave her the twenties. "Girlie-cues," she said softly, sounding kinda sad, actually.

Lying in bed that night, though, all I could think of was my gold coin, shining against my skin. Paper money wasn't the same. *Very true,* Annabelle murmured. *Now, did you know a capful of bleach keeps cut flowers from wilting? Seems strange, I know, but—* She went quiet. *Ahhhh. She's coming.*

"Who?" I whispered.

Never you mind.

"Gah!" Someone yelled outside my window and there was a *thump-thumpity-thump*. I got up on my knees to look out. In the dim light of the half-moon, I saw somebody hunched at the foot of the hillside steps from Vilma's, rocking back and forth like they hurt themselves—fell down the steps, I figured.

"Is that Vilma?" I whispered to no one.

Yes. Go to sleep, Petunia.

Vilma stood up and limped around the corner of our house, heading for the river.

I lay down, closed my eyes, brain buzzing. What was Vilma doing, sneaking to the river in the dead of night?

Stay inside, Petunia.

No chance.

I got up and crept out the back door in my T-shirt and shorts and sandals, and crouched behind a tree.

Oh, Petunia. Go back to bed.

I tiptoed across the road and knelt behind a rosebush. Vilma was heading for Table Rock.

Stay down, Petunia. Do as I ask for once.

Vilma stood at the end of the rock, her back to me, and called out something I didn't understand.

I heard . . . *sploosh*, like a fish jumping.

The river went quiet, quiet . . .

And shattered into a million drops as something exploded out of the water into the air. It was something impossible, something huge, shining bright green and red. It whooshed straight up, flapping these ginormous bat wings to go high, higher, slapping me with wind and that spicy, swampy scent.

Whump-whump-whump. That noise, like the wings of a thousand eagles.

This was the most wonderful, awful, amazing, horrifying thing that ever happened to me.

CHAPTER SEVEN

Distant Thunder

The creature swooped and soared over my river. Red belly, the rest of it shiny green—exactly like the tattoo we saw before on Vilma's wrist. Dark spikes lined its back, almost to the tip of its tail.

A dragon. A *dragon*.

I could barely breathe, because this moment suddenly seemed like my whole reason for living. Sure, the thing was big and scary, but also it . . . I don't know exactly how to say this. It's just that . . . it *worked*, the universe at its best. This was how wings were supposed to bend and unfold and beat the air, this was how you designed a body if you wanted it to glide through the sky like a seal through the ocean. For one minute out of my whole life, I saw why a person would write poetry.

And of course right then the dragon swooped up, flapped madly, and crash-landed like a clumsy cormorant in the middle of the river, back feet first.

Okay, so that could've been better.

The dragon moved smoothly through the water towards Table Rock, where Vilma was waiting. It sidled up against the rock, and then—oh then—Vilma climbed up to sit between the spikes at the base of the dragon's neck. It eased away from the rock and flapped its wings. The two of them lurched into the sky.

Vilma Bliksem—our new neighbor we gave brownies to—flew away on a dragon. They flew right over where I was standing in the half-moon light, and Vilma looked right at me. I crouched down too late. No way she didn't see me. But I was too blown away to worry. "Annabelle," I whispered. "Did you see that?"

What a beautiful creature.

"I'm going nuts."

No, Petunia. But it's time to go back to bed.

I couldn't, not right away. I made it to our front porch, wondering if kids ever had heart attacks. I sat there, breathing, watching the moonlight on the river, slapping black flies.

Jeez'm.

Dragons are real.

Finally I went in—it was two o'clock in the morning.

I climbed into bed next to Herbert the mouse in a hat, Florinda the My Little Pony clutched in my hand. Thunder rumbled in the distance, somewhere south over Bangor. A comforting sound, normal.

Next morning, I thought I dreamed it all. Until I saw the grass stains on my knees.

Dragons are real.

The radio was on in the kitchen. When I went in, Janice was at the table, frowning into her yogurt, not eating. "Weird, weird, and strange," she said.

I froze. "You . . . you saw it?"

"*Saw* it? No, you dingo, I *heard* it. On the radio."

Okay. All right. Okay. "Heard what?"

"They said there was this wacko thunderstorm. Last night. It was exactly one block in area and it hit exactly one tree."

"Huh." That did seem odd, but I mean . . . I saw a *dragon*.

"The tree fell into a shop window, destroyed it." She spooned up some yogurt but didn't eat any. "It was his window. The gold dealer's. Altin's."

Okay, yeah, that was weird.

I cooked my oatmeal. Janice ate her yogurt.

I didn't tell anyone about the dragon. For two seconds, I thought about telling Hillyard—it came out of the river, after all, so he'd probably have a theory. But no, he'd think I was a looney tune and so would everybody else. And it would be even worse if they *did* believe me—nobody would let a dragon stay in our river.

That beautiful creature. No, I couldn't tell anyone.

Feeling a serious need for almost normal human conversation, I made sure I met Hillyard in front of Vilma's house. He had on a Grateful Dead T-shirt and striped jeans in six to twelve colors. "You look exhausted," he said.

"Thanks a lot," I said. "Strange jeans."

This, of course, was exactly when Vilma's front door slammed open and she stuck her head out. "Child."

Should I run? The woman was a million years old and wearing pink-flowered L.L.Bean pajamas. Still . . . dragon rider.

She glared like nobody's business. "Do not come to clean today."

Oh, man. "Hang on," I said to Hillyard. "I'll be right back." I don't know what got into me, but I ran up the front steps and right past Vilma into her living room. I needed that money.

She whirled to face me. "Get out."

I took a breath. "Is this because I saw the dragon?"

Oh, jeez'm, she about broiled me with her eyes. "Get out, I said."

"Please. I need the money. You said I haven't learned to betray yet. I really haven't."

Silence. More eye-broiling. "I will know if you tell," she said.

"I won't. I swear."

"And you ask me no questions."

"Sure, sure, whatever." How could I not ask questions? There was a *dragon*. But I remembered that gold coin in the palm of my hand, so pure, so shiny, and the seven twenty-dollar bills. "I won't say another word about it. I promise."

"All right. Clean the house. Like last time. Do not be late."

"Who the heck was that?" Hillyard asked when we got going.

"Vilma Bliksem. Moved in about when you did. I clean for her. She pays me."

"My mom won't let me have a real job. She says I have to be a child some more."

"Must be nice."

Aw, Petunia.

"I don't feel sad about it," I said. I was strong, I was independent. I was *not* going to Cousin Betty's.

If ever I needed my last look at the river, today was the day. Hillyard stopped too. I breathed deep, smelled the damp, felt the moisture on my face. Dragons were real.

Hillyard said, "Like a glittering seam of stars."

I stopped breathing. "What?" That was from Anna-belle's river poem.

"River runs free, river runs free, like a glittering seam of stars."

I faced him. "Where did you hear that?"

"It's from this poem my mom says all the time. You love the river. Don't you think it's a glittering seam of stars?"

"Yeah. I do."

We turned back to the river and breathed.

I sat with Hillyard at lunch, at the far end of the Rachel-and-Taylor table. They ignored us. We ignored them. Sitting at the same table as Rachel and ignoring her was about as peculiar as seeing a dragon. This one time in third grade Sally Anderson didn't invite either of us to her birthday and me and Rachel got all huffy and sat by ourselves at lunch for a whole week. It was horrible but we had each other.

Now I had Hillyard. Who thought the river was a glittering seam of stars.

And in that river was a dragon. I saw it. Rachel and Taylor didn't.

Ha ha. I win.

* * *

After school, I dropped my backpack at home and knocked on Vilma's door. "Do the front room," she said, and locked herself in the spare bedroom before I could think of a way to ask about the dragon without seeming to, you know, ask about the dragon.

The living room furniture belonged in the dump, except for maybe the new coffee table with the raccoon feet. But I opened the windows and rolled up the rug and scrubbed the wooden floor and polished the wood furniture. I even put bleach in water and made the walls all white again.

As I scrubbed, Annabelle recited the poems she'd included in the Guide and told me how to make chocolate fudge cake. I loved having Annabelle in my head.

"How do I ask her about the dragon, Annabelle? I really want to see it again."

I'm sure the feeling is mutual. Better to wait and see if she brings it up, Petunia.

Vilma came out after a couple hours. "This is much better." She sounded surprised.

"You should throw out most of this furniture," I said, mostly to prove I could talk about something other than dragons.

She smiled the pencil-jab smile. "I have something new." She went back in the spare bedroom and returned with a footstool. The top, where you'd put your feet, was all gray-and-white fur. Raccoon fur, I realized when I looked closer.

"You have kind of a thing about raccoons," I said.

"Nasty creatures." She put the footstool near Mrs. Wittingham's easy chair that had the stuffing coming out. She eyed me a minute, then said, "Come drink tea."

O-o-o-okay. This morning she was doing the eye-broiling thing. Now we were having a tea party?

I kinda eased into the kitchen and sat down at Mrs. Wittingham's old table, and Vilma gave me one of Mrs. Wittingham's white mugs, which were really, *really* white because I bleached them before. Her mug had raccoon ears sticking up out of the handle.

I couldn't think of anything to say that wasn't dragon-related. I had so *many* questions.

She peered at me so intently she gave me the creeps. "You are sorrowing for your dead aunt."

Huh? When did I say anything about having any aunt at all, let alone a dead one? "Uh . . . yeah. She died last August."

Vilma nodded vigorously. "She was a good woman. Not like your sister. Your sister is mean to you."

"She's not really mean. She's just busy and . . . and sorrowing."

"Mean," Vilma insisted. "Sisters have an obligation

to each other." She took a sip of tea. "To ignore that obligation is a betrayal."

"Who's been talking about us, anyways?" Rachel's aunt Dana at the store? Dave Pelletier?

"Not your business." Which it kind of was. How unfair was this: I couldn't ask about the dragon, and now I couldn't find out who was dishing dirt on us.

People do gossip, you know. It's one of their less attractive qualities.

Vilma pushed back her chair and grabbed our mugs, dumped them in the sink. She told me to leave, and that was that. Anyways, thanks to me the place reeked of bleach.

The next day, Thursday, it reeked of chickens.

Because a rooster and two hens were living down cellar.

CHAPTER EIGHT

The Henhouse

Vilma and I stood at the bottom of the cellar stairs, watching a speckled black-and-white hen peck a hole in a box marked "Grandmother Wittingham's porcelain teacups."

"Do Mrs. Wittingham's kids know you're keeping chickens down here?" I asked.

Vilma shrugged. "Only three now." She gave me a whole new smile, kind of Grinchy. Made my backbone shiver. "I'm sure there will be more."

The hen gave up on the box and made a beeline for my feet. I stepped up on the bottom stair to make it harder to peck me, but that wasn't what the hen wanted. She turned her head sideways so she could stare at me with a beady eye and started squawking like she had something to say, flapping her wings, doing the laser stare first with one eye, then the other. And she kept hopping and flapping like she wanted to fly but couldn't figure out how.

A brown hen and a red rooster hustled over, and pretty soon all three of them were hopping and flapping at the foot of the cellar stairs. They were like a windup toy display at the mall. There was something weird on the rooster's head, but I couldn't get a good look.

"What's the matter with these things?" I moved up another stair.

Vilma kicked at the rooster. "Go away, stupid birds." She watched them scurry off, feathers flying. "They do not like being chickens."

"What do they want to be instead?" I never heard of an animal not wanting to be exactly what it was. The chickens huddled a couple yards away, squawking at me. They all pooped at once, like a protest.

"You can't keep chickens in here," I said. "It's unsanitary."

"I will use bleach as you did."

"That'll probably kill them."

Vilma started a low growl. The birds ran to the farthest end of the cellar and tried to hide behind a box marked "yard sale stuff."

I settled my feet on my stair, ignoring the way Vilma's eyebrows were jutting out, because I was getting this amazing idea. "If you fix up the shed, they can live out there."

"They do not need a shed. I will put them outside."

"They'll get eaten by a fox or something."

She frowned. "Show me."

We went out the bulkhead steps. Bizarro Bird heard my voice and rushed out from beneath the shed, but when he saw Vilma he squawked and flopped back under. "What kind of bird is that, do you know?" I asked Vilma.

She smiled her Grinch smile. "Lark."

Didn't look like any lark I ever saw.

The shed was in bad shape but basically strong. Whoever made it knew what she was doing, like Mim and Annabelle.

And me. "I could fix this," I said. "I could turn it into a henhouse. For as many hens as you want." An excited, glimmery feeling whooshed over me.

Vilma looked doubtful. "You can do this by yourself?"

"I'll get help if I need it." Mim, I thought. Mim will be all over this.

Vilma nodded. "We will buy everything now. You can fix it tomorrow."

It had to be almost five. "It's too late today. And I have to figure out what I need. Tomorrow's Friday and then it's Memorial Day weekend, so plenty of time to work on this."

I left Vilma muttering to herself about foxes, but I didn't even care. I was so excited I barely saw the steps as I went down. Another chance to escape Cousin Betty— if anything was going to wipe that dragon out of my mind, this was it.

Well, maybe it wasn't *quite* wiped out of my mind. I mean, *dragon*. Maybe I'd wander down to the river later.

"Why are you so happy?" Janice asked, coming in while I was unwrapping a frozen dollar-store pizza I found under the ice cubes in the freezer. I guess I was humming to myself.

"Got a new job," I said. "I'm fixing up Vilma's shed for her."

"Big fancy deal."

"I bet I can get more jobs like this. I bet I can work all summer doing this stuff."

"Dream on, Petunia."

"Don't call me that."

"Petoooooonia," Janice said, and headed for the stairs.

Someone should step on that girl. Let me at her.

Jeez'm, Annabelle.

I bounced around the living room, pretending to dust but actually sending vibes for Mim to come home *now*.

When she finally opened the kitchen door, I threw my arms around her before she even put down her briefcase. "I have the best news," I shouted.

She let me drag her to a chair at the kitchen table.

"Mim." I used my deepest and most important voice. "Ms. Bliksem needs a henhouse."

She blinked.

"I'm going to fix up her shed for her! And I know what to do, because of helping you and Annabelle with the shop. It needs siding and a new roof, and maybe boxes inside for the hens—got to look that up online."

"Donna. Girlie-cue."

"This'll be great!"

Mim put her hands on my arms. "Donna, I'm selling the tools. The truck too. I put an ad up online."

I waited for her to say she was joking. But she never joked anymore.

"Mim, I'm bringing in money."

Man, she looked sad. "Donna, I love that you're trying to help, but that hundred and forty you girls gave me pays about a tenth of what I owe every month. If we get a good price for the truck and the tools, I think we'll be okay for a while."

"And I won't have to go to Cousin Betty's?"

She actually reached up and ruffled my hair, which she never does. "Maybe. There's still the problem of what to do with you when Janice and I are at work. We'll see."

"I'm not a baby."

"No, you're not. But, Girlie-cue, you're too young to spend the whole day here all by yourself and we don't have the money for day camp or anything."

"I'll get a babysitting job around here." But we both knew I couldn't compete with the older kids.

"You know what?" Mim said. "The tools probably won't sell right away. Go ahead and fix up the shed for Ms. Bliksem. But do it fast. Once the tools sell, they have to go."

Mim went upstairs to change her clothes. I plunked down at the kitchen table.

"Not so chirpy, hey?" Janice strolled in. "When's supper?"

"Shut up."

"Let me give you a big sister's word of insight. Stop getting your hopes up and you'll be better off." She stretched her arms over her head and yawned. "That's what I did."

"Yeah. And look how happy you are."

"Face it, Petunia. We ain't going to be happy."

CHAPTER NINE

Hippie Senior

Never made it down to the river—I spent the whole time before I went to bed making lists of what I thought I needed for the henhouse. Annabelle made suggestions from the Guide, but I didn't think Vilma's henhouse needed fleur-de-lis stencils around the doorway.

I figured I'd measure the shed first thing after school, then—oh, jeez'm—let Vilma drive me to Allen's Building Supply.

I didn't even ask Mim if she wanted to help me. She was out in the kitchen typing and typing and typing—I knew what she'd say. But as I sat there thinking how I'd do everything—design nest boxes, board up the walls, shingle the roof—I started to wish I wasn't in this all by myself.

I actually didn't build that much of the carpentry shop, when you thought about it. And Vilma was going to be hovering over me the whole time, wasn't she? A person who rode a dragon.

I'm with you, Annabelle whispered.

For once, that wasn't much help.

"What's the matter with you?" Hillyard asked next morning as we said goodbye to the river. "You aren't even insulting my clothes." He was wearing a red-and-purple tunic and a blazing yellow scarf, wrapped around his neck about a hundred and fifty times.

"I dunno," I said, but then somebody behind us yelled, "Child! Child!"

Petunia, I think she means you.

"The name's Donna," I muttered. Vilma was out front of her house in her flowered pj's. "Do not be late," she called. "We must buy wood and such."

"I'll be there as soon as I can." I didn't sound all that polite.

"Good morning." Hillyard bowed.

What a wonderful boy.

Vilma muttered something and stalked back to her house. I was feeling worse and worse about my great idea.

We got going again. "Why are you buying wood and such?" Hillyard asked.

"I'm turning Vilma's shed into a henhouse." I told him all the work the shed needed.

Hillyard whistled. "You know how to do all that?"

"I helped my mom and my aunt build a workshop."

He re-whistled. "Wow. My dad helped me build a birdhouse once for Boy Scouts. But I never did anything that big."

I was starting to feel a little better about myself.

"I love chickens," Hillyard said. "We had them back at the farm."

Of course they did. But also . . . "Did you have a henhouse?" I was getting another idea.

"Yeah, of course. How many chickens she got?"

"Three now. But she says she'll get more."

"We had forty."

Fact: It about killed me to share my money.

Another fact: I didn't want to do this alone. "Can you draw me what your henhouse looked like inside? I looked online but I'm still not sure what to do. I'm figuring six or eight hens."

"Ours was way too big. I'll come with you after school and draw something new."

So I really had to pay him now. "I'll share the money. It's minimum wage." Lying's okay when you really need the cash, right? My stomach wasn't so sure.

Hillyard bounced on his tiptoes. "This is so cool. Can I come with you to buy the lumber too?"

At recess, we looked up lumber sizes on a school computer. I also looked up the lark, just for fun, but the only one that looked anything like Bizarro Bird was the European skylark, which had the same brown Elvis-y hairdo. It lived in Europe, Asia, and North Africa, so that couldn't be my little guy, obviously.

Obviously, Annabelle murmured.

When Hillyard wasn't looking, I googled "river dragon." I got a ton of pictures, but none of them looked like the one in our river.

Google said they were "mythological." You can't always trust the internet.

Rachel walked by with Taylor and Mei Xing, but all I saw was the back of her head. After school, Hillyard and I walked behind Rachel and Sarah all the way to Vilma's. I made Hillyard slow down so we didn't catch up. I was starting to get used to Rachel hating me, which made it even more depressing.

I reminded myself that I saw a dragon. I was going to see it again, too, no matter what Google said about myths.

At Vilma's, I measured things while Hillyard plunked himself down on the grass to start sketching a floor plan with nesting boxes and roosting perches and shelves underneath to catch the poop. It was a lot more complicated than I would've expected a day ago.

But this was Hillyard, whose mom was a biologist. He liked things complicated.

Vilma loomed over his shoulder. I could tell she was making him nervous. He erased, drew again, chewing his lip. "I think you need insulation for winter but I don't know what kind. And I'm not sure how the perches went. I'll text my dad."

"Wait . . ." I started, but he already pressed send. Great, I thought. His dad can't keep a job of his own so now he's going to horn in on mine.

Personally, Annabelle murmured, *I'd welcome the reinforcements.*

Mr. and Mrs. Martin showed up ten minutes later. You could see right away where the hippie genes came from: Mr. Martin had a ponytail like Hillyard's, except his was red and curly. He had on a leather vest like Hillyard's, too, plus a woven hemp bracelet and a turquoise scarf wrapped around his neck a bunch of times. But he also had a tool belt around his waist, all dirty from use—exactly what a tool belt is supposed to look like, I had to admit.

Mrs. Martin must've come right from the university, because she had on nice black pants, a red silk tunic, and flat dressy shoes, her brown hair up in a bun.

She beamed at me, just like Hillyard. "Hello. You must be Donna."

I bowed like Hillyard. Why, I couldn't tell you.

"Wonderful that you two are taking on this project," Mrs. Martin said. "And you're a river girl, Hilly says." Hillyard made sort of a choking sound.

He talked about me at home. Also . . . *Hilly*.

Mrs. Martin held her hand out to Vilma. "Hello. I'm Sheila Martin. This is my husband, Boyce." Mr. Martin waved, but he was more interested in Hillyard's drawing.

Vilma looked at Mrs. Martin's hand like it was a snake. "I am Vilma Bliksem."

Mrs. Martin lowered the hand and gave Vilma the "interesting specimen" look I saw on Hillyard's face a few times. "Did you *snarl*?" she asked. "I never heard a human do that before."

"Terrific drawing, Hill," Mr. Martin said. "But you need more ventilation." The two of them hunched by the shed door while Hillyard erased, drew, erased.

Memories of Mim and me and Annabelle working together on the shop stabbed at me, especially when Mr. Martin put his hand on Hillyard's shoulder in an absent-minded kind of way.

Finally, Mr. Martin and Hillyard came over to where we were. Hillyard was all happy. "We got it figured out," Mr. Martin said, then looked at me. "I don't want to butt in, but would you like me to take you and Hill to Allen's in the truck tomorrow morning?"

On the one hand . . . yeah, butt out, Hillyard's dad. On the other hand . . . no driving with Vilma. I decided that was worth something, so I nodded.

The three chickens were under the shed with Bizarro Bird all this time. While Mr. Martin and I made our plan for the morning, Mrs. Martin was on her hands and knees trying to coax them out, getting her nice pants all dirty. Now she made a choking sound and backed off like she saw a skunk. "That rooster has humanoid ears!"

I remembered thinking before that something was strange about the rooster. I got down next to Mrs. Martin. Sure enough, the bird had teeny, perfectly formed pink ears on either side of his feathery head.

"What the heck?" Mr. Martin crouched down too.

"A special breed," said Vilma.

"Where did you get it?" Mrs. Martin looked totally disgusted. "I researched our chickens. There is no such thing as a chicken with humanoid ears."

"There is now," Vilma said. "A mistake, I admit."

Mr. Martin patted his wife's shoulder. "It's okay, hon," he said. "You can't know everything." She shot him a look, but she didn't say anything more.

After the Martins left, I ran in the house after Vilma like I was brave or something. "You owe me for three more days of cleaning," I said. No more dubbing around with a little money here, a little money there. I needed serious dollars and I needed them now. "You can pay me in gold if you want. Save your cash."

Maybe she'd think she owed me three coins for three days. But even one would be fine. So shiny, so pure.

Careful, Petunia. Craving this gold is a sickness.

Vilma came back with a hundred and eighty bucks. "I will keep my gold," she said, giving me a serious stink eye. Still, she gave me three times what she owed me. I didn't say anything.

Is bilking an employer considered proper behavior, Petunia? I'm curious.

"You want me to go live with Cousin Betty?" I whispered.

She didn't have an answer for that.

My stomach hurt.

I stashed the money in my room, saving up so I could hand Mim a honkin' big pile of cash.

Next morning, we filled Mr. Martin's truck with building supplies till we barely had room for our feet in the cab, and got to Vilma's by nine o'clock.

She was outside, pacing. "How long will this henhouse take?" she asked Mr. Martin as we were unloading the truck.

"I'm not the boss here," he said. "Ask Donna." Okay, that was nice.

"We'll go fast as we can," I said. "Maybe a week or two?"

Vilma growled.

Mr. Martin stuck around to help, and I was actually pretty relieved. Except for one thing. "Um," I said. "I can pay . . ."

Mr. Martin put up his hand to stop me. "This is your job, and Hill's," he said. "I'm just his dad."

I turned my back on them so they wouldn't see my face. I couldn't decide what I was feeling: Was I sad because Mim wasn't helping too, or happy I didn't have to share any more of my money?

I decided to go for happy.

Which lasted right up until we needed saw-horses and things, and we went down to our shop. Hillyard told his dad everything was for sale.

By the time we finished nailing the last board of the day, Mim was done at the bakery and she came through the yard on her way home, carrying a bag of two-day-old bagels the bakery gave her.

I introduced everybody.

"Thank you for helping Donna," Mim said to Mr. Martin.

She kept patting the boards like they were pets, said we did a nice job. Mr. Martin went down to the shop with her to talk about the tools and how much she wanted for them, which made me feel small.

Hillyard stayed to help me pick up.

I took a deep breath. "Uh, I couldn't have done this without you and your dad."

"It's fun."

"Plus . . . it's good to have a friend with you when you deal with Vilma." There. I said the f-word right out loud.

His ears got reddish, but what he said was, "No problem. See you tomorrow." He really was a good guy.

CHAPTER TEN

Shopping with Vilma

Monday afternoon, we found out about Vilma and bad luck.

The shed was four-fifths done, and the chickens were spending the night in it. Work went real well on Sunday, and on Monday morning, Memorial Day, even Mim came up for an hour. I think she couldn't stand construction going on without her. She impressed the heck out of Mr. Martin, gliding up and down a ladder with a nail gun that seemed like it was part of her hand. She's got the moves, you know?

Vilma came out to growl at us a few times. Every time she did, the three chickens ran away screaming. "Smart chickens," Mr. Martin muttered.

Bizarro Bird ran under the shed. Something under there made a noise that sounded almost like a giggle. A minute later, something zipped past the corner of my eye. When I looked, it wasn't there.

It was three o'clock, the parents had left, and Hillyard and I were taking a break, when Vilma came out again. "I must go to that food store." She gestured towards Main Street. "You two will come with me."

Rachel always, always worked at the store on Monday holidays. "We're real, real tired," I said. "Anyways, why do you need us?"

"I wish to try new foods. You will advise me."

Hillyard groaned and flopped backwards on the grass. "I'm totally too tired."

Vilma said, "I will pay you more money. Half a day."

"Each?"

Her eyebrows stuck out so much you almost couldn't see her eyes. But she nodded.

I stood up. "C'mon, Hillyard."

"No way," he said. "I don't need money that much. Plus, you said she's a scary driver."

"I am a good driver," Vilma said. "Better than last time."

"You got a license?" I said.

"Ha. That woman at the registry place, she thought she was so smart." I took that as a no.

Still, she'd been driving for a week or two. She had to've learned something, right?

I told Hillyard, "Friends don't let friends risk death by themselves." He sighed like a whale and got up.

I got in the front seat as a show of confidence, and Vilma started the car without any trouble. We drove along for, like, three blocks without running up on the curb or anything.

But then she turned the School Street corner, and for reasons I still can't explain she floored it, howled up the street at a million miles an hour, ignored the red light, and squealed around the corner to storm up Main Street, almost going right past the store. I yelled, "Stop! There it is! There it is!" So of course Vilma slammed on the brakes and yay for seat belts—my shoulder felt like somebody kicked it, but at least I didn't go through the windshield. We swerved into the lot, lurched into a space at this nutty angle. I rubbed my shoulder, hoping it wasn't dislocated or something.

"We are here." Vilma screeched open her door and set off for the store entrance.

Hillyard was gripping his seat belt strap with both hands. "That was exciting."

When we got inside, there was Rachel at the cash register. I stayed on the other side of Vilma, who booked it to the butcher's counter. "I want to try . . . that." She pointed to a huge turkey.

"Um, do you even have pans?" I asked. "Potholders?

A cookbook? It's a lot to cook a whole turkey. It takes hours. You have to baste the thing."

Vilma glared at the turkey like it called her a name. "I don't want to do any of that."

Don't push it, Petunia.

I looked at Hillyard. "Frozen dinners," he said.

We got Vilma a couple turkey dinners and some mac and cheese and a Salisbury steak. We got her baby carrots, figuring that was something she could eat without cooking. She already knew about eggs—she boiled them, she said—so we got some of those too.

You're probably wondering who the heck could live so long without cooking anything except hard-boiled eggs. Well, yeah, we were kinda wondering that too. Trouble is, you can't find out anything when somebody's growling at you all the time.

And if you know the person rides a dragon . . . well, maybe you don't want to ask too many questions.

I thought about booking it for the parking lot rather than going to the cash register, where Rachel was smiling like a beauty queen at some guy with, like, six canvas bags of groceries hanging off his arms.

You're going to run away? Does this mean you can never buy food here anymore?

Annabelle had a point.

Rachel didn't notice me and Hillyard at first—Vilma

was sort of overwhelming, being so tall and ferocious-looking, and she was blocking us from sight. But after she rang Vilma up, Rachel smiled this tense smile and said, "Oh hey look, the Loser League."

Vilma frowned. "What is this league?"

Rachel pointed at me and Hillyard. "Them. They're the Loser League."

When we were eight, Rachel dumped a whole cup of orange soda on Taylor's head because she said my ears stuck out like an elephant. Now look at us.

Vilma noticed the expression on my face, which must've been pathetic. "This thing she said, this Loser League, it hurts you?" She took that little leather book out of her satchel.

I almost ignored the question—somehow, admitting you're hurt makes you seem like even more of a loser. *You're not a loser,* Annabelle whispered. *So why worry if you seem like one?*

I looked up at Vilma. I nodded.

Two seconds later, the giant rack of cigarettes behind Rachel groaned and tipped away from the wall, dumping all the cigarettes on the floor and landing on top of them with a crash. Missed Rachel by half an inch. All six bags hanging off that guy's arms split at the bottom as he was going out the door and all his stuff rolled into the parking lot. Guess he liked this fancy soda in green glass bottles. Too bad, because they broke.

Rachel yelled and ran to help him.

Hillyard's eyes were the size of donuts. Vilma pushed her cart out the door, humming under her breath, right past Rachel and the fancy-soda disaster.

On the ride home, I barely noticed Vilma's driving.

What the heck happened back there?

I wondered when you'd start asking questions.

When we got to her house, Vilma turned off the motor and said, "That girl. You want me to make her sorry?"

"Um, excuse me, what? Make her *sorry*?"

"Bad luck."

"What do you mean, bad luck?" Hillyard asked from the back.

"You saw. I can give her bad luck."

Silence, except Hillyard was breathing pretty loud and it was freaking me out, so finally I blurted, "Who are you?"

I believe the question is "what" rather than "who."

Jeez'm.

Vilma screeched open her door. "Come inside."

I couldn't decide if I wanted to go inside with a who that might be a what.

You'll be fine, Petunia.

"Donna," Hillyard whispered. "Think it's safe to go in there?"

"There's something I never told you." By now, I was

pretty sure Hillyard would believe me. "There's a dragon in the river. Ms. Bliksem rode it. And she has a ton of gold coins. But don't say anything—I promised not to tell."

Long silence, then: "Cool," Hillyard said. "Let's get in there."

We put away the groceries, showed Vilma where to find the directions on the frozen dinners. Sat down at the kitchen table, hands clenched.

Vilma peered at me, then Hillyard. "What I am telling you now, you must tell no one."

We nodded.

"I am trusting you like family." She said that sort of growly, like it was a threat.

Oh dear.

"Like *family*?" Frankly, what with Cousin Betty and all, I already had enough family, thank you.

Hillyard opened his mouth and shut it again.

"Especially you, Donna," Vilma said. "You are like a little sister. We understand each other."

Petunia, be very, very careful about this.

Vilma leaned forward, lowered her voice. "I am going to tell you my secret now."

I nodded. So did Hillyard.

"I"—Vilma straightened her spine—"am a thunder

mage." She paused like we were supposed to cheer or something.

"A what now?" Hillyard said.

"A *thunder* mage. A wizard who calls thunder. There are not many of us left and not many know of us." She smiled her pencil-jab smile. "Except gold dealers, like that man who had a tree fall on his shop."

I remembered how scared Mr. Altin was when he saw the dragon on Vilma's wrist. "Why do gold dealers know about you?"

"Our gold is legendary."

Ask yourself, Petunia . . . legendary for what?

"Why is it legendary?" Hillyard asked.

"Because of my ancestors' skill. They served kings who loved gold, so they made it for them."

"They *made* it?" No way, I thought.

"They used lightning." Vilma sighed. "But our skills have faded, and no one knows how they did it. All we have left is the gold itself."

That coin, shining in my grimy hand. "It's still around? Gold somebody made with *lightning*?" Oh, jeez'm. "That gold you gave me, was it . . . ?"

She didn't say anything, just looked at me.

Jeez'm crow.

We went quiet, Vilma staring at her hands. Hillyard

fidgeted. Finally, to break the silence, he asked, "So, how do you call up thunder?"

Vilma blinked, like he woke her up. "I must ride a dragon."

I waited for Hillyard to act surprised, and when he just sat there I kicked him. "Ow!" he said. "Uh. A dragon? You're kidding!"

The whole mood changed. Vilma smiled, like, a real smile. "Indeed. A dragon. There are not many left, but some live in the river near where we . . . I mean, *I* . . . made our . . . my home. This river of yours, it's like ours, magical because it crosses a ley line and has rough water. It is good for a dragon."

Huh. So it was true about ley lines. But magical—really? I thought about how good I always felt beside the river. *A glittering seam of stars,* Annabelle whispered.

It occurred to me what Vilma just said. "Who's *we?*" I asked. "You said 'we.'"

Another mood change. "Betrayal," Vilma growled.

We waited.

"My younger sister," she said at last. "We lived together in the forest. The people came to us for luck or curses, farmers came for rainstorms. Sometimes a *bad* storm, to destroy an enemy." Her voice dropped to a whisper. "Not like our ancestors, who made gold for kings. But it was a good life. For years . . . a hundred or two, I never counted."

Okay, exactly how old *was* Vilma Bliksem?

She had the third-saddest face I ever saw, after Mim's and Janice's when Annabelle died. "A man came to our woods to cut trees. Sarika . . . she *married* him." Vilma slammed her hand on the table so hard I about jumped out of my skin. "Treachery! Betrayal! She said nothing would change between us. But she moved out of our cave—our beautiful cave, with its walls of glass and gemstone—to live with him. Treachery!"

Hmm. So now she's here, with her family's gold. Don't you wonder why?

I really didn't feel like asking about that.

Vilma got up to kick the refrigerator and roared, "BETRAYAL!"

Hillyard leaned over and whispered, "Did she say people came for luck or *curses*?"

I thought about the cigarette rack almost hitting Rachel. Maybe we should get the heck out of there.

But I needed Vilma's money, didn't I? I had to stick this out. Anyways, something about the Johnson's Food Mart disaster was bugging me. "So . . . at the store. Before the cigarette rack fell down—you took out that leather book you have. You held it in your hand."

She turned, her eyebrows jutting out. "My book is not your business."

Okay. All right. Okay.

She came back to the table. "That girl, The Loser League one. She was your friend once."

"Yes." The day Annabelle died, Rachel came over and stayed with me all day. I couldn't cry, but I also couldn't move. We sat in the TV room and watched Animal Planet.

"She betrayed you," Vilma said softly. "I can make bad luck. Make her sorry."

I could feel Hillyard eyeing me, kinda stern. "No, no," I said.

But you really do want to make Rachel sorry, don't you? Annabelle asked.

And before I could stop it, my brain whispered, *Yes*. It was just a thought. What harm could that do, right?

Wrong.

Vilma watched me, eyes narrowed. Out of nowhere, she uncorked that Grinch smile and winked.

All set, Annabelle said.

Vilma gave me another wink.

I opened my mouth to say something, make sure we all knew I really didn't want to hurt my ex–best friend.

"Come meet my dragon," Vilma said. "Tonight. Sunset."

"Really?" Hillyard jumped to his feet. "Awesome!"

I definitely should say something, I thought.

But I didn't.

CHAPTER ELEVEN

Margily

When I walked into the kitchen at home, I was feeling bad I didn't make sure Vilma left Rachel alone. I didn't feel bad enough to go back up there, though.

Did part of me think Rachel deserved a little bad luck?

Maybe.

Mim and Janice were sitting at the table, a wrinkled letter between them. Janice looked like she could bite the head off a snake.

"Hey," I said.

Janice pushed her chair back and stomped out of the kitchen. Then she stuck her head back in and said, "You could've told us how bad it was. We're not children,

Nancy *Jane*." And she was gone again. Mim's mouth was so tight you couldn't even see her lips.

"What's going on?" I said.

"Sit down, Donna." She was white as the refrigerator, with these dark blue circles under her eyes.

I sat. "What's the letter?"

"It's from my loan officer. I got it Saturday. If I don't make a serious payment they're going to call in our loans. All of them."

"What does that mean?"

"I gotta sell those tools to Hillyard's dad right away. Wish he'd buy the truck—that's the most money."

"What happens if . . . if we can't pay?"

"We could lose the house."

I touched the letter with one finger. I felt the house around me, watching over us, keeping Annabelle alive in all her carvings and paintings.

Mim put her hand on mine. She *never* did that. "Girlie-cue, you have to go to Cousin Betty's this summer. I can't worry about you being home alone. I don't have the brainpower."

"If I get lots of work . . ."

"Sweetie, you won't have any tools. And most people won't hire somebody your age. Cousin Betty says she'll buy you school clothes. It's really nice of her. She's trying to help us." She squeezed my hand. "It won't be so bad."

"That's not what Annabelle used to say."

Mim pulled her hand back. "Janice said I don't have any idea what's going on in your lives." She peered at me. "Is anything happening to you other than the henhouse?"

Well, I thought, my best friend hates me and at sunset I'm going to sneak out and meet a dragon. "No. Nothing's happening."

"Okay, Girlie-cue. I'm sorry."

She went out to the living room to get on the phone. A minute later, I heard her talking about the tools—to Hillyard's dad, probably.

I tried to do homework, but there was no room in my head for anything but two facts: I was about to meet a dragon, and I was maybe losing the only place I ever lived.

I'd help if I could, Petunia. I don't want you to go away and leave me behind.

"Me neither," I whispered.

Later on, I knocked on Mim's door and Janice's but nobody wanted supper. Spreading peanut butter on a stale bagel made me feel worse.

By the time sunset rolled around, it was pretty clear nobody would even notice if I left the house. I went out the back door just in case, so Mim wouldn't hear.

The sky and the river were this amazing dense blue-gray color, blushing red at the edges. The air was soft and sweet, birds chirping, the rapids sighing in the distance. In another mood, I would've loved it.

Hope is everywhere, Petunia.

Yeah, right.

Hillyard waited in the road, all hunched up and tense. He had on red sequined sneakers, about the worst thing you could possibly wear to mess around by a river. Except maybe for too-big sneakers that might trip you into the water, like the ones on my feet. We'd have to be careful out there.

"I hope this dragon's not, like, dangerous or something," Hillyard said. "But I guess it'll be worth it."

Vilma stood at the far end of Table Rock, arms crossed, feet firm. We stayed on the riverbank because . . . well, duh. Dragon.

She took a deep breath and called across the water in some other language.

Something downriver made a *splooshing* sound.

"Whoa," Hillyard said. A huge, spiky, bright green back broke the water in a smooth motion, disappeared, reappeared closer.

"What's that smell?" Hillyard whispered, and sure enough, I caught a whiff of that spicy, swampy scent.

The spine-spikes submerged. The river went quiet. I held my breath.

"Gaaah!" Hillyard yelled as the dragon exploded out

of the water, opening its giant wings. It flap-flap-flapped up into the air, green and red scales shining, and circled Table Rock, *whump-whump-whump.*

Something moaned in the bushes behind us, but I couldn't be bothered to turn around. I couldn't believe how perfect this creature was, the way it beat the air with its wings.

"I think I'm going to cry," Hillyard said. "Never saw anything move like that."

The dragon circled one more time and did its clumsy landing. Waves flooded the shore. (Hillyard swore and danced, trying to keep his stupid sequined shoes dry.) The beast glided towards us, head and neck above water. It touched the river bottom, walking till its chest butted up against Table Rock.

Its massive head gleamed emerald in the fading light. The eyes about killed me to look at—serpent-slanted but this intense blue, electric and cold.

"French cobalt," Hillyard muttered. "Got a tube of it—"

"Shhh." I moved out on the rock. I wanted to get close.

The head towered over us, even taller than Vilma, who was at least six feet tall, you remember.

"This is Margily." Vilma reached up to pat the snout, the one part that didn't have spikes. "River dragon." She jutted her eyebrows at us. "Tell no one about her."

The dragon eyed us. I meant to say hello. All I could

manage was "He-o-ooow," kind of a tongue-less moan.

Vilma scratched the side of a massive nostril, crooning. The creature snarled, showing off three rows of scary-sharp teeth, a good six or ten inches long. Vilma whipped her hand away.

"Dragon," Hillyard whispered behind me. I tried to remember what it was like not to know about giant, emerald-colored flying reptiles.

Hello, children. The voice was pleasant, musical . . . and inside my head. "Ohhhhh," Hillyard moaned. I clapped my hands over my ears, as if that made any sense, because you'd think I'd be used to head-voices by now.

Especially this one. But I was too freaked out to focus on why.

"It's talking in my head," Hillyard whimpered.

It, the lovely mind-voice said, *is a she. And standing right here and quite capable of conversing with you.*

Hillyard kinda shrank. "I'm sorry. I didn't mean to be a ninnyhammer."

Ninnyhammer. Such a scrumptious word. Also, I love those shoes.

"Th-they're from the church thrift shop," he said. Like a forty-foot dragon was going to go shopping.

"A dragon talks in your mind," Vilma said, though we pretty much figured that out. "To one person or many, as she chooses."

Before we proceed further, the mind-voice murmured, *perhaps the unpleasant older sister would be pleased to join us?*

Huh? I looked wildly around, but I didn't see any unpleasant older sister. Well, except for Vilma.

The rosebushes behind us, though—they were thrashing like a hurricane. Somebody stepped out, and I figured out who moaned when the dragon first showed up. She wasn't moaning now—in fact, she jammed her fists on her hips, Wonder Woman–style. "Leave Donna alone, you . . . you lizard."

"I'm fine, Janice." I did not add: *Anyways, what do you care?*

The dragon—Margily—reared up her gorgeous head, blasted steam out of her nose—I could feel the heat from where I stood. *Whom are you calling a lizard, you ill-tempered adolescent?*

Janice gave her head a shake. "Get out of my mind. Lizard."

No chance. Margily narrowed her eyes. *By the way, that boy with the black hair. You should stop dreaming about him. It's never going to work out.*

Janice clamped her hands over her ears, which of course made no difference at all. "That's mean," I said, trying not to notice that my stomach was a clenched fist.

Because this voice was *so* familiar.

"You can read all our thoughts." Even in the dusk, I could see Hillyard's ears were beet red.

Of course. The corners of the dragon's mouth curled up, sort of a smirk. *And as to "mean," she did call me a lizard, after all.* The smirk widened into a gentle smile. *Petunia, dear.*

"Hey," Janice snapped. "That's what Annabelle called you."

It took a minute. Then reality rushed over me in a tidal wave. I doubled into a crouch. Annabelle was dead and I was the stupidest person in the world.

I had her with me for, what, three, four weeks? She shared housekeeping tips, told me I was okay, like she always used to. Even when I thought it was only me, talking in my own head, even when it sounded strange, like nobody I knew, still it was a warm hand at my back, comforting, encouraging.

All along, it was this . . . this reptile.

I sat down hard on the rock. "You took Annabelle stuff out of my head and said it back to me." I hated how my voice sounded, a little kid with a boo-boo.

"No kidding?" Hillyard said. "She was talking to you before?"

"Weeks. I thought it . . . I don't know what I thought."

"You thought it was Annabelle." Janice sounded as bleak as I felt, a shell full of tears. She had her hand in her jacket pocket, clutching at something.

Hillyard stuck his chin out at the dragon. "That's cruel. How could you—"

"I beg your pardon," Janice broke in. "But who is this kid with the shoes?"

Hillyard turned and gave Janice his dorky little bow. "Hillyard Martin. Pleased to meet you."

Janice gave me a "what the heck?" gesture. I said, "He's fixing up Ms. Bliksem's henhouse with me." I was too tired to get up.

"Oh right," Janice said. "The big excitement Mim stomped all over the other day."

One good thing—Janice was making me forget about the Annabelle situation. "Why are you here? Does Mim know I sneaked out?"

"You are a complete dweeb but if you creep down to this river at night I'm going to make sure you're okay. Not eaten by a giant lizard, for example."

I am not a lizard. And I do not eat children.

"So you say. Lizard."

The huge snout eased down till it was a foot away from me, cobalt eyes gleaming. *I am sorry if I hurt your feelings, Petunia.*

"Don't call me that." Her breath was a little fishy.

To my astonishment, the dragon's big blue eyes filled with what looked like tears. *Your thoughts of your Annabelle were so strong, I entertained myself by giving her back to you. Who could have guessed I would come to like you so much? Admire you, in fact—you are not a whiner, are you, dear?*

"Unlike some I shall not name," Vilma muttered.

The dragon's tears dripped onto the rock, raising puffs of steam. *I didn't mean to raise false hopes.* She shot Vilma a quick side-eye, then looked back at me. *In fact, you are the only good thing about this place.*

"If you don't like it"—Vilma smiled that mean, Grinchy smile—"why don't you leave?"

Margily snorted. *I have to go where you go, old woman, and you know it.*

"Why is that?" Hillyard asked.

I couldn't believe Hillyard was standing there making conversation with this creature. "Annabelle," I whispered, and covered my face with my hands.

A mage cannot make thunder without a dragon. So they weave a spell and bind us to them. We cannot break free.

"That's terrible!" Hillyard sounded shocked.

"You love to make thunder," Vilma huffed. "And you can't do it alone either."

That does not mean I want to be bound to one mage for time immemorial.

"A dragon is nowhere without a mage's skill," Vilma said.

You must know a human's mind to affect their luck. You need the dragon's telepathy to guide you.

"Pfft," Vilma said.

When we traveled across the ocean, who was it who

found the ley line we followed? You would be under the waves without me.

"You don't belong in this river," Hillyard said to Margily, in Mr. Science mode. "Who knows what kind of foreign algae you got on you, and now it'll spread all over the place. You're like a northern pike."

I beg your pardon.

"Somebody put them in the river system and they're eating up the fish that belong."

I do wish to be at home, in my own sparkling river. This one has magic enough, but it also has . . . what did I hear you and your mother call it? Mercury? In any case, I resent the comparison. A pike of all things.

The cobalt eyes turned back to me, a sad lump on a rock. *Come for a ride, Donna. I want to make it up to you for . . . for Annabelle.* She turned to Hillyard. *You may come too, pike boy.*

"No, thanks." I wanted nothing to do with her.

"I don't go up in the air." Hillyard crossed his arms, like he was protecting himself. "One time, I puked on the Ferris wheel and it splattered all over some guy's head."

"I will keep you safe," Vilma said.

Hillyard didn't look convinced. "It was the *kiddie* Ferris wheel."

Don't worry. I would be in control.

"You would not," Vilma snapped. "I am the leader."

Margily chuckled in my head. *The mage is only as good as the dragon.*

"I do not need your help to fly. Remember that, lizard."

"Whoa," Hillyard said. "You can fly by yourself?"

Vilma looked proud. "Yes, I can."

No, she can't. Not without her book in her hand and not for long distances.

"Quiet," Vilma snapped.

Margily turned her head to look at me. *All her magic is in her book, you realize.*

Vilma slapped the dragon's snout. "Worm. I said to be quiet."

She wrote it all in there herself, when she was just a girl. All mages rely on their books. Important to know, really.

Vilma stomped her foot on the rock. "Silence! Or I . . . I will make you sorry."

Margily blew a little burst of steam out her nose. *Just try it, old woman.*

It was almost dark. Exhaustion dropped on me like snow falling off a roof. "I have to go home now." I wanted to be in my bed, looking at Herbert the mouse with the hat.

Please. A brief ride. Margily's snout moved closer, as if she were whispering. Her spicy, swampy scent filled my whole head. *Seize the day.*

Annabelle used to say that all the time. Also—

Gather ye rosebuds while ye may. Margily's mind-voice was so quiet, so gentle.

"You're taking that from my head," I whispered. "Annabelle's gone."

It will be good for you, Petunia. Things that seem big down here—they become very small when you're in the air.

"Don't call me Petunia," I said.

"So, I guess you probably know how to not drop people," Hillyard said.

If I planned to drop a person, it would be Madame Vilma. Or this older sister Janice. Certainly neither one of you.

Janice was on the rock, hauling me to my feet. "You're not going up there, Donna."

I almost let her drag me away. But . . . Annabelle. She would never pass up a chance like this. I shook her off. "I'm going. For Annabelle."

"I-I might stay right here," Hillyard said. "I don't want to get these shoes wet. Plus, there's the Ferris wheel puke thing."

Hillyard, Margily said, *don't be a ninnyhammer. I love your shoes. I won't get them wet.*

Hillyard stood there a second, then lunged forward, not giving himself time to think, hoisting himself up on her back between two spine-spikes, a leg on each side like he was riding a pony at the fair.

Vilma pointed at the space in front of him, between spikes in the shoulder area. "You go there," she said to me. I swallowed hard and put my foot on Margily's folded wing.

"Donn-a-a-a-a . . ." Janice made a grab for my arm but I squirmed away and made it to my seat between spikes.

Close up, Margily's scales could've been jewelry, each one a slightly different shade of bluish green, gleaming like the abalone shell Annabelle kept on her windowsill. The spikes were darker green, smooth as glass but warm to the touch.

"Beautiful," I whispered.

Margily looked back at me, arching her neck like a cat being scratched. *I know.*

Vilma leaped onto Margily's wing—who knew she could move like that?—and took a seat at the base of her neck. Barely waiting for Vilma to settle herself, Margily waded away from the rock and flapped her giant wings. We rose from the water.

And then, oh then.

A rush of sweet spring air in my face. The river sank beneath us, shining silver-blue in the twilight. Margily's wings pumped, heading up steep—it felt like they might pitch us off. Behind me, Hillyard gave a loud moan. I wrapped my arms tight around the spike in front of me, praying he didn't puke and me neither. Everything went cold and damp as we passed through a little cloud, then we burst out into deep blue, my little town spread out below us, surrounded by woods. Streetlights winked. The school's parking lot lights flickered on.

Joy, Margily said.

I wondered what would happen if somebody looked up.

They will tell themselves what suits them.

Vilma began chanting in her language. As we flew north, scudding over thick Maine woods, she raised her arms, palms up towards the sky. Warm, humid air rushed up from the ground.

Clouds billowed around us, and Margily sped up, flying around and around in a tight circle. The hair rose on my arms and head, like I had my hand on the static ball at the science museum. "Wahoooooo!" Hillyard yelled behind me.

Annabelle would've loved this. For a second, I felt like she was with me—not her voice, not this dragon in my head . . . just *her.*

Joy, Margily said again.

Vilma clapped her hands and . . . *Bam!* A flash of light half blinded me, and *bang!* A blast of thunder made my ears ring. Margily kept circling, faster, tighter. The air erupted in flashes and crashes.

A minute later, Margily leveled out and blasted into clear air and moonlight. As we zoomed towards home, I snuck a look back over my shoulder and saw a thunder cloud raining and crashing and flashing over some poor village.

Don't worry. They looked like they needed the rain.

As we headed back, I realized Margily was right. Up

here, everything else seemed small. Everything felt possible. We'd figure out the house. There had to be a solution.

I felt like nothing bad could happen to me ever again.

Landing was maybe a little more exciting than I wanted, Margily flapping hard, her back heaving, the dark water rushing up, and the final belly flop almost threw us all in the river. When I stepped back onto Table Rock, I almost fell over. But I didn't.

Janice wasn't there to see us land. I hoped she wasn't calling the cops. Or telling Mim.

Good night. Come back anytime.

"Good night." I looked into Margily's cobalt eyes. "Thanks for the ride."

She nodded slowly, dignified.

"I didn't puke," Hillyard said.

I didn't go in the house right away. I stayed on the front porch and breathed deep, clinging to the last shreds of how it felt to fly through the air on a dragon.

Sploosh! Whump-whump-whump!

Margily flapped into the moonlight. She glided, tilted, swooped, happy as a swallow, then slid out of sight beyond the trees.

Good night, Petunia.

I almost wasn't mad at her anymore.

Almost.

CHAPTER TWELVE

Rachel Is Sorry

When I got inside, Janice was sitting on the living room couch, arms folded, like she was waiting up. "So. You survived."

"Yeah." I headed for the kitchen door.

"You could've died. I was actually worried, even though we can't afford you. Incidentally, Mim knows you sneaked out."

I turned on her. "I never in my whole life tattled on you."

"I didn't tattle. She was down here looking for us when I got in."

"What'd you say?"

"I said I was at Michelle's and you were doing homework with the kid with the shoes. She sniffed my breath to see if I'd been drinking. But she totally trusted you, because you're Little Miss Reliable."

"Donna?" Mim's footsteps creaked down the upstairs hall towards the stairs.

"Books," Janice hissed.

I zoomed out for my room, grabbed some book, made it back before Mim got downstairs.

Mim looked like somebody smudged under her eyes with charcoal. "I'm glad you have someone to study with, Girlie-cue. What were you working on?"

I looked at the book in my hand. "Um. Biology." I opened at the bookmark, saw "Chapter Six, Human Reproduction," and slapped it closed, but not before Janice caught sight of it.

"You were studying human reproduction with a boy?" She had this smirk on her face, which made no sense considering she'd covered for me in the first place.

I thought fast. "That's the next chapter."

Mim sniffed the air. "What smells spicy?"

Janice raised her eyebrows at me, smirk still in place.

Jeez'm. "I . . . candles. Mrs. Martin burns candles."

"That's nice." Mim turned back to the stairs. "I'll have to thank her for letting you come over."

My spine froze. If she checked with the Martins about tonight . . .

Janice shook her head at me like I was *so* pathetic. "Oh, I wouldn't, Mim. It'll make Donna look like she's a loser little kid." She dropped her voice so only I could hear. "Instead of a loser big kid."

Mim smiled. "Wouldn't want that." She hauled herself up the stairs. "Good night, girls."

"Night, Mim," I said.

Janice whispered, "You owe me big." To my surprise, she followed me to my room and leaned against the doorframe while I changed for bed. "So," she said at last, "what was it like?"

"You should've come," I said. "It was amazing. It was like . . . it was Michelle's dad's rope swing at the lake, times a thousand. And they made a thunderstorm."

She shook her head. "This is too weird. I don't like it." She pointed a finger at me. "Don't you go up on that thing again. It's too dangerous."

"You care?"

"Of course I care." She pushed herself off from the doorframe. "You're a major source of gold for this family."

Next morning, Hillyard was waiting in front of Vilma's, jigging up and down, all excited. "We rode on a dragon!" he yelled when I was barely in sight. "She liked my shoes!"

"Keep it down. The neighbors'll think you're nuts."

He's sweet, Margily murmured. *And don't you love what he's wearing?*

Hillyard had on the red sequined shoes, of course—he probably was planning to wear them every day now. He had a maroon scarf wrapped around his neck and tight lime-colored jeans under a too-big New England Patriots jersey.

"Colorful," I mentioned.

"Yeah." He was practically skipping. "Margily likes color."

Rachel wasn't at the lockers when we got to school, which was fine with me.

Did I remember about Vilma's bad-luck magic? No, I totally did not.

It felt horrible not having Annabelle anymore, but watching the other kids goof around the hallway that morning, I realized what I did have: I knew about something amazing and it was swimming around in the river but also in my head. And they had no clue.

Made me stand up straighter and jostle back when I got jostled. I was almost starting to feel better about having Margily in my life.

I went to the office to see if I could get my locker moved and explained how Rachel and I were enemies now but they told me I had to stick it out. "You'll be friends again before you know it," said Mrs. Herrick, the school secretary. Yeah, right.

Turned out Rachel wasn't in school at all, and nobody

knew where she was. Last class of the day, Taylor and Sarah and Mei Xing sat together behind me and whispered.

"She's not answering her phone." That was Taylor.

"Mrs. Herrick called the house," Sarah said. "No answer there either."

"Maybe something happened to her and her aunt and they're in the hospital." Mei Xing sounded all freaked out.

Hard to believe—I *still* wasn't thinking about Vilma. But just before the bell rang at the end of the day, Hillyard whispered, "You don't think Vilma did something to Rachel, do you? You said *not* to do something, right?"

"'Course it's not Vilma. I told her no," I said to him, weaving through kids.

But my mind did say *yes*, didn't it?

Margily went, *Um.*

I stopped dead in the doorway, blocking traffic so everybody said, "Jeez, Donna" and huffed past me.

"What, Margily?" I whispered.

Have we mentioned the transmogrification spell?

"Transmogrification? What's that?"

Well, let me just say there seem to be a couple of new hens.

Oh.

"Is Margily talking to you?" Hillyard whispered over my shoulder. "Is it about Rachel?"

"We gotta get to Vilma's," I said.

We were out the door and down the street in two and a half minutes, at Vilma's in five, panting. Her car wasn't there. "Look for a couple of new hens." I pelted into the backyard, trying not to trip over the extra toe room in my sneakers.

"New *hens*?" Hillyard said. "What does that have to do with Rachel?"

"I don't know. Let's just look, okay?"

We hunted and hunted but it was just the same three chickens. It was only when we gave up and trudged down to my yard that we found the new hens: a white one with red speckles standing at the bottom of the hillside steps, and one beside it with a glossy black head and tan body.

The black-and-tan one cocked her head exactly twenty degrees. She stamped her foot at me.

No, no, no, no . . . I sank down on the steps. "Rachel?"

The hen gave an angry squawk and ruffled her feathers.

To make sure, I said, "If you're Rachel, turn around in a circle."

She waddled right around three hundred and sixty degrees, squawking the whole time. Then she snuggled up close to the red speckled one, which clucked nervously. "Um," I said. "If you're Rachel's aunt Dana, you turn around too."

Oh, jeez'm.

This really happened. And I did it. To *Rachel*, the girl who once dumped orange soda on Taylor for me. And her nice aunt. The Rachel-hen stabbed my sneaker with her beak, luckily hitting the too-big part where my toes weren't.

"This isn't our fault, you know," Hillyard told her, sitting down next to me. That's when I realized I was the only one who knew how much it *was* my fault. Other than Margily, of course. And Vilma.

"Yeah," I said. "Vilma got mad because Rachel insulted us." I mean, that was where it all started, right?

The Rachel-hen *floomp*ed down, her head drooping. I guess it's depressing being a hen.

The three original weirdo chickens flapped down the hill and lined up next to Rachel at our feet, squawking. Bizarro Bird joined them. Oh, man. "Anybody who's supposed to be human," I said, "turn around in a circle."

All six twirled. "Whoa," Hillyard said. "Who are the other ones?"

I thought about the complaints I'd heard from Vilma over the past week and a half. For example, the "greedy little man" who sold her the car. "If anybody is Dave Pelletier, turn around in a circle."

Yep. Bizarro Bird. Elvis hairdo and all.

I thought some more. "Mr. Altin?"

The rooster with the ears.

If you recall, Madame Vilma has not yet received a driving license.

"Anybody here from the Registry of Motor Vehicles?" The black-and-white speckled hen squawked excitedly and turned around in a circle.

"Who else did she deal with?" Hillyard said.

I should perhaps mention that she doesn't really like pink but it was all they had that fit her.

The flowered pj's. "Anybody from the L.L.Bean outlet?" The brown hen turned around like a clumsy, squawking ballerina.

Annabelle's Guide said nothing about a situation like this.

"You see, I made the bad girl be a chicken."

I about jumped out of my skin. Vilma stood at the top of the granite steps. All six birds screeched and ran over to huddle by Mim and Annabelle's old workshop. Vilma grinned at me in a way that actually seemed real.

"Uh, thank you," I said. "We're not mad anymore, though, so you can turn her and her aunt back now."

The grin vanished. "You do not like what I did for you?"

Hillyard's forehead got all wrinkled. My face heated up, even though I wasn't even lying yet. "Um, yes. It was . . . very funny. But she's my friend—*used* to be my friend—and her aunt's a nice lady. Please turn them back."

The other birds squawked.

"The others too," I said. "Please."

Vilma's eyebrows twitched together. "This is my artistry. It is not to be undone by a child's whim." Her mouth trembled. "I did this for you, because you are a good girl. And you refuse it? I trusted you like family." She narrowed her eyes. "Tell me, how did you find out the chicken was the bad girl?"

I didn't answer. I wasn't about to tell Vilma about Margily helping us.

Vilma looked at Hillyard. "You know things about chickens. How do you cook them?"

The birds shrieked and ran off to the little bit of woods between us and the neighbors. Vilma shrugged. "They won't get far." She went back to her house.

"Donna." Hillyard's voice was so quiet it about made my skin crawl. "Did you ask Vilma to make Rachel sorry?"

It was not possible to look at him.

"No," I said. "I didn't."

Hmmm. Interesting answer, Petunia.

Guess she didn't let Hillyard hear that, because he

said, "Yeah, it didn't sound like something you'd do."
Now I did look back at him. He was smiling at me.

I rubbed my belly, which hurt like heck. "Hillyard,
you are a good friend."

He got real interested in his feet.

"C'mon," I said. "We gotta find those birds before
Vilma does."

He got up. "What'll we do with them, though?"

Good question. "Well, we could put them in our
workshop. Or maybe that's too close—how about
yours?"

"My parents will think we stole a bunch of chickens.
They'll never believe what's really going on."

Good point. Focus, Donna. "Okay. So. We need to
stick them someplace safe, but it has to be with somebody who won't think we're nuts."

"And who knows Rachel well enough to get the whole
head-cocking, foot-stamping thing," Hillyard added.

*You need someone who believes in magical beings such
as myself and Madame Vilma. And pixies, of course.*

"Pixies?" Hillyard and I said in unison.

*Of course. When you see movement in the corner of
your eye and you look and nothing's there, that's how you
know they're around. Quick as a thought, pixies.*

Hillyard looked like he ate a toad. "Are they . . .
everywhere?"

No, no. They live on ley lines where they intersect with rivers. Especially places like this, where rapids stir up the magic that's latent in any river. When we followed our ley line to get here, we stopped because of the pixies—we felt we'd be welcome.

"Annabelle said pixies had to bathe in river water to stay magical," I said.

Such a wise woman. There's really nothing that special about magic, you know. It's simply the transformation of one thing into another—good luck to bad luck, motion and moisture into a thunderstorm. In some ways, it simply enhances what's already there.

This transmogrification of humans, though—that is wrong and I do not approve.

"When this is over," Hillyard said, "I am *so* apologizing to Uncle Patrick about the pixies."

They are very pleased about those little houses on the shore, by the way, Petunia. People don't usually think of their comfort. They enjoyed the sweets you left too. And the water.

"They're living in our little houses?" Oh, Annabelle. I wanted to run right down and look.

Couldn't, though. Because I had a pretty good idea who had to help us. And I didn't like it one single bit. "We gotta talk to the B-team. Sarah, Taylor, Mei Xing— they believe in all this stuff. But I don't know if they'll help—they'll call me a loser."

"They'll help if it's Rachel," Hillyard said. "Anyway, sticks and stones."

That was something, coming from Hippie Hillyard. "Don't you care what people say about you?"

He shrugged. "I care. It makes me feel bad sometimes. But who lets other people run their life?"

I thought about the way I treated him all year. "I'm sorry about calling you Hippie Hillyard."

He looked me in the eye. "It's okay." We both knew it wasn't.

What a lovely boy. Now, get moving before Madame Vilma comes back.

Didn't take long to find six birds freaking out together under a honeysuckle bush in the woods. "We're taking you to Sarah," I told the Rachel-hen. "She's closest."

The four other chickens and Bizarro Bird crowded around, cheeping in this pitiful way. "We can't bring all of you," I said. "First we need a plan. Stay here and we'll come back for you later."

I reached for Rachel. She squawked with an attitude and scuttled away from me.

"I know how to carry hens," Hillyard said. "Better let me do it." Rachel let out another long, furious squawk, so I guess that was an even worse idea.

What a ninnyhammer. Does she want to be caught?

"Shut up, Rachel," I said. "Vilma will hear you. And

you have to let somebody carry you out of here, unless you want her to get you." The other hens clucked at Rachel and she let me walk up to her.

"Keep your hand under her and her wings pressed to her sides," Hillyard said. "Let her nestle in the crook of your arm."

A minute later I had this heavy, feathery creature under my arm, cozy like a teddy bear. Except the creature was Rachel.

And she was a chicken.

Jeez'm.

CHAPTER THIRTEEN

Tortilla Chips

We were all ready to head out when we saw Vilma up in her dooryard, probably looking for the birds. There was no way she wasn't going to see us. Rachel trembled in my arms.

"We have to distract her somehow," Hillyard said.

"Margily," I whispered. "Can you do something?"

Yes. Hide yourselves.

We crouched down and waited. Nothing happened at first but then Vilma gave an angry yell and booked it down the hillside steps into my dooryard. She hustled past my house and down to the river.

I told her I have found a way to break our bond and go home without her. A lie, of course. I am learning so much from you. Now run! Hurry!

We ran down our road and hung a right onto Smith

Point, where the houses are practically *in* the river, just below the rapids.

"So we have to see Sarah now." Hillyard sounded hoarse.

"Get it together, Hillyard." I wasn't feeling much better about this than he was. At least Sarah wasn't Taylor. I led Hillyard to the kitchen door and knocked.

Somebody was crying. We could hear through the door. Lots of somebodies.

When Sarah opened the door she was a wreck, hair all messy, eyes all red, cheeks all wet. "What do *you* want?"

"Your parents home?"

"They're at work. Duh."

"You said your mom was doing, like, a First Nations thing up north." Hillyard's ears turned red, I guess because now we knew he eavesdropped on Sarah at lunch.

"Okay, *you're* not creepy at all," Sarah said. "And it's not a 'thing,' you oaf, it's called a powwow."

Hillyard looked like he got a brain freeze.

And then, jeez'm, Taylor came up behind Sarah, also messy and red-eyed. Then Mei Xing. Thirty-three-point-three percent of the girls' basketball B-team, having a sob-fest.

"Are you guys crying?" I asked. "Why?"

"Why aren't you?" Taylor said. "Rachel's *disappeared*."

That's when I realized I didn't do one bit of planning about how this conversation would go. I looked at Hillyard, he looked at me, and we blurted, "This is Rachel." I held the chicken out in front of me.

"How dare you?" Mei Xing shoved Sarah out of the way. "Rachel's not answering her phone and you're making some stupid *joke*?"

Rachel gave a long, despairing squawk. Don't know where I got the courage, but I shoved through the door before Sarah could shut it. I put Rachel down. "Do something they'll recognize, Rachel."

She ran to a cupboard and pecked at it till I opened it up. She dragged out this huge bag of tortilla chips.

She pecked at the fridge and then this jar of really gross cheese-jalapeño dip on the bottom rack on the door. "You're kidding me," I said, but she stamped her foot so I got it out and opened it for her.

The B-team were frozen like statues.

Rachel dragged the bag of chips over to Sarah and pecked at it. Sarah looked at me all wide-eyed. I said, "Maybe open it and give her a chip?" Sarah put the chip down on the floor next to Rachel, who stamped on it to break it up, used her beak to dip one piece into the cheese. She tried to eat it but I guess it was too gross for a chicken, because she started hacking and coughing.

"She needs water," Hillyard said. Mei Xing filled a bowl from the tap and put it down. Rachel lunged at it.

When she stopped coughing, the hen looked around at her teammates with beady little eyes full of hope.

Mei Xing shook her head. "Nope. Nope."

"You could've trained that chicken to do all this," Taylor said.

"You think we figured out where Sarah keeps her tortilla chips and told a *chicken* about it?"

"Maybe," Taylor said defensively.

Rachel gave a little huff and stamped her foot once, twice, three times. She cocked her head exactly twenty degrees.

Thirty-three-point-three percent of the girls' basketball B-team looked at Rachel, at me, at Hillyard, back at Rachel. Sarah said, "Stamp your foot for how many Lord of the Rings figures I have."

Rachel hit her little clawed foot on the floor one, two, three times, on up to thirty-three. Sarah saw the looks on our faces. "What? That includes orcs. They're organized by size."

Mei Xing burst into tears all over again. "Oh, Rachel!" She went down on her knees and threw her arms around the black-and-tan hen.

"Careful not to squish her," Hillyard said. Mei Xing squeaked and let Rachel go.

Taylor looked like she hit her head. I totally understood—this stuff is hard to deal with when it's real life instead of TV. She started to say something, but Mei Xing got in there first.

"How the heck did this happen?" she asked.

We all sat down at the kitchen table, Rachel pressed against Taylor's leg, and I told them about the thunder mage living next door with a dragon and sacks of gold and a magic book that could change people into birds. I told them about Dave Pelletier and the other bird people. I said Vilma got mad when Rachel insulted me and turned her and her aunt into chickens. And we needed to hide them until we figured out . . . something.

"I bet you're making all this up," Taylor said. "To get back in with us." Rachel let out a squawk and pecked Taylor's big toe.

"Okay, okay." Taylor jerked her foot away. But she never took her eyes off me and, man, she looked mean.

The other B-teamers were all shiny-eyed. "This is awesome!" Mei Xing said. Rachel squawked again. "Except for you being a chicken, of course."

"I *knew* there was strange stuff going on in this town," Sarah said. "I mean, a *dragon*, Taylor. I bet you'll know what breed it is." She beamed at me. "Is it still in the river?"

Why, yes. I'm right here. And it *is a* she. *How do you do?*

Everybody slapped their hands over their ears.

"Margily's telepathic," Hillyard piped up helpfully. "That's her name. Margily." Sarah went to the sink and glugged down a giant glass of water. It's weird having a dragon in your head.

"We're talking to a *dragon*?" Taylor whispered.

Yes. No doubt we will meet in person soon.

"Ohhhhhh." For a second or two, Taylor forgot about not believing me. She went bright red, she was so excited. "What color are you? How many feet do you have? Do you breathe fire?"

"Um, hello?" I said. "Could we focus? We need to hide Rachel and the other birds. Then I have to figure out how to change them all back."

To my surprise, everybody nodded.

Except Taylor, of course. "How are *you* going to change them back? You can't do magic, can you?" Dragon or no dragon, she still thought I was a loser.

Sticks and stones, right? Plus I was thinking about this for the last hour or two. "I'm going to get Vilma's book. It's got all her magic in it."

Oh, no, no, no. Petunia, I cannot stress enough the astronomical dangers involved in touching the book of a thunder mage.

Sarah made a *snerk* sound. Still not used to having a dragon voice in her head, I guess.

"What else are we supposed to do, Margily?" My voice sounded shrill even to me. "Ask her nicely? I tried that and it didn't work." Rachel gave a little cluck, like she understood how desperate I was.

Long silence. Then: *You may be right.*

Okay then. "How do I get it? Seems like she always has it with her."

Only when she leaves the house. You know where she keeps it when she's home.

"I do?" I thought about it. "Ohhh. The spare bedroom—the one she didn't want me to go in. I figured that was because she keeps her gold there."

That too.

"So she'll be *home* when we look?" Hillyard said. "How the heck . . . ?"

"We have to distract her again," I said. "Make her leave the house."

I'm afraid I've run out of distractions. She won't believe me a second time. Petunia, if you insist on doing this, you must be very, very careful.

"Why does it call you Petunia?" Sarah whispered.

"Long story."

I am a she, not an it. No need to be uncouth.

"I'm sorry," Sarah whispered.

Mei Xing looked like she wanted to start crying again, watching Rachel the hen peck at the tortilla-chip pieces on the floor. "We need to help," she said softly. "We'll help you get the book."

The B-teamers looked at one another. Taylor swallowed hard. "Yeah. We'll distract the witch—"

Mage.

"Mage. We'll distract her."

The other two nodded, faces solemn.

"Okay. All right. Okay," I said. "But first, we need to get the other birds."

The B-team nodded, eyes wide. Fantasy was getting real.

Sarah said we could put the birds in the empty house next door. "The owner left the key with us in case somebody wants to look at it but nobody ever does because of the ghosts."

We decided Hillyard would take the B-teamers to get the other hens, the rooster, and Bizarro Bird. Before they left, Sarah handed me a battery-powered lantern. "Watch out for the ghosts. I guess maybe they're real too," she said.

Actually, it's most likely not ghosts. Pixies love to take over deserted old houses, especially so close to their river.

"Pixies," Sarah whispered. "Co-o-o-ol."

As I carried Rachel next door, she shook like she was freezing to death. "I'm sure pixies love hens who are supposed to be people," I said.

The kitchen was dark and cobwebby. Also weirdly cold, even though it was warm outside. There was no furniture—instead, there were pink flower petals all over the floor.

Something zipped past me, too fast to see. When I put Rachel down, she pressed herself against my ankles. "Hello?" I yelled. "Pixies? We're friendly."

Pixies don't respond to yelling. In fact, they don't respond to much.

"What do they do all day?"

Something flicked past my side-eye.

They dance. Gather flowers for nectar. Play, if it's sunny, sleep if it's not. They like to help humans, although I'm afraid their efforts are not always helpful.

A pink flower appeared out of nowhere and floated to the floor in front of Rachel. She gave a miserable cluck.

"Chill out," I said. "I think they like you."

The pixie house kitchen door crashed open way sooner than I expected. Hillyard and the B-team lurched in carrying chickens and slammed the door behind them. Bizarro Bird clung to Hillyard's shoulder.

"Man, that was close," Hillyard panted. He put down the rooster with the ears, Mr. Altin, and the B-team put their hens down, and pretty soon there was a chicken party going on, everybody huddled together and clucking. Bizarro Bird made it from Hillyard's shoulder to the floor on his own—guess he was learning to fly, finally. He hopped over to join the hens.

"How'd it go?" I asked.

Taylor was grinning like a nutcase. "It was *so cool.* We cut through the woods and after we got the chickens we had to go behind that lady Mrs. Wells's house and she came out and started yelling at us for trespassing and the witch came out in front of her house to see what the screaming was all about."

Thunder mage. She is a thunder mage.

"We hustled back through the woods, then we split up and zigzagged to throw the witch off. It was *awesome.* Like Magic Milton and the Grail Sprites on TV."

"She means the mage," Sarah said quickly before Margily could start griping again.

"Yeah, yeah, the mage," Taylor said. "When do we get to meet you, Margily? I love dragons."

One thing at a time, child. You have more than enough to do right now.

Bizarro Bird flapped to the top of a cabinet, took off to fly around the room like an expert.

"Mr. Pelletier?" He was flying awful well for a used-car salesman.

He landed on the counter and let out a stuttery call.

"Huh," Hillyard said. "Is he forgetting he's human?"

"Mr. Pelletier," I said, "if you understand what I'm saying, turn around three times."

He ignored me.

Rachel turned around three times, stamped her foot, and cocked her head twenty degrees, squawking the whole time.

I've been wondering how to break this to you.

"Margily?" I said. "What do you mean?"

If one of Madame Vilma's victims isn't unmogrified in time, he or she will forget about being human. It may already be too late for your Mr. Pelletier.

"He's been a bird a lot longer than Rachel," I pointed out.

Unfortunately, the process goes faster for young people. Much faster. Four or five days, I'd estimate.

"You mean Rachel could be a chicken *forever*?" Mei Xing gasped.

"Well, not for*ever*," Hillyard said, "Realistically, a chicken only lives seven or eight years."

The B-team wailed like one person.

"We have to *do* something," Sarah whispered.

"Donna needs to get that book *now*." Taylor slammed her fist into her hand.

"Can you really undo the spell?" Mei Xing asked me, and there was this suffocating pause because we all knew I couldn't even dribble a basketball.

Takes a spell to undo a spell. Donna is right—reading the book is the only hope.

Taylor started pacing. "So, we have to get the wi—I mean, the mage. We have to get her out of her house. How do we do that?"

I closed my eyes and imagined Vilma running out her front door because . . . because of what? A bunch of basketball players?

Well, why not? "I have an idea." They all paid attention, even Taylor this time. "You could do something with a basketball."

"Perfect." Hillyard bounced on his toes. "They could thump it off her house. Or her car! She'd hate that. It would make her *really* mad."

The B-team looked at one another and the birds at our feet and did a group swallow. Taylor slapped her hand on the table. "We'll do it. Let's go."

But we couldn't, because Taylor's and Mei Xing's cell phones rang at the same time. "Oh jeez," Taylor said. "It's six o'clock. I gotta go home."

"Me too," Mei Xing said.

"But . . . but we have to do this *soooon*," Sarah moaned.

Hillyard and I looked at each other.

"We're going to have to sneak out and do it tonight," I said.

"Oh, man," Hillyard groaned. "Sneaking out *again*."

"No big deal," Taylor said. "Me and my sister sneak out all the time."

Another thing. You have to pluck a feather from each bird. So you can make the book's magic work from a distance. Otherwise you have to be touching both the birds and the book when you say the words.

"Let me do it," Hillyard said. "I know chickens." He grabbed Aunt Dana and stroked her until she relaxed and shut her eyes, grabbed a feather, pulled up real quick. She barely squawked.

Me and Sarah caught Mr. Altin, the brown feathered L.L.Bean lady, and the speckled lady from the Registry of Motor Vehicles. Bizarro Bird—Mr. Pelletier—was harder, because he flitted all over the place, but Taylor and Mei Xing finally caught him and he got plucked too.

Rachel gave an unhappy squawk.

"Hey," I said, "if getting a feather pulled out is the worst thing that happens to you, we're doing good."

Somewhere in the house, I swear somebody giggled.

CHAPTER FOURTEEN

Keep Away

We all met at midnight in the woody section of our road, wide-eyed and twitchy. Taylor, Sarah, and Mei Xing had basketballs. Everybody had head-lamps, though nobody turned them on yet.

"I'm going in the house with you," Hillyard whispered to me. "You can't do that alone."

I didn't argue.

"Okay, let's do this," said Taylor. "We'll spike the ball at her house and her car. And we'll play keep-away when she comes out."

Do not let her take anything from you. That's one way she effects transmogrification. She likes to be holding on to you when she says the spell, but a lock of hair or even a piece of clothing will help her.

Oh jeez'm. That must've been why Vilma stole Mr.

Altin's hat that time. "Seriously," I said. "Be super careful." Even you, Taylor, I thought.

And Petunia, you must be extremely careful what you say aloud when you have Madame Vilma's book in your hand. Best not to speak at all. Not until I tell you to.

"Why not?" I asked.

It's a long story. Just do as I say.

The B-team went to Vilma's front yard. Hillyard and I went to the back. I was so scared my hands and feet were freezing.

Vilma's kitchen light was on.

Out front, Taylor yelled, "Two-four-six-eight, the B-team is really great!" I think she made that up right then, because it was even stupider than a real cheer.

Something smashed into Vilma's car with a hollow, metallic sound.

Something boomed against her house.

Vilma roared from indoors and, a moment later, from out front.

"Ohhhh, I hope she doesn't catch anybody," I whispered.

Somebody else was hollering out front too. "You hoodlums!" Mrs. Wells screeched. "At this hour?"

"Oh, man, what if Mrs. Wells calls the cops?" Hillyard said.

"We can't worry about that now. Let's go!"

We raced in Vilma's back door and through the house to the spare bedroom, pulling the door almost closed behind us.

Remember, Petunia, when you have that book in your hand, DO NOT SPEAK.

Something was humming inside the little desk in the corner.

"Is that . . . ?" I whispered.

Yes. Remember what I said about speaking.

The thumping against the front of the house continued—the basketball. The B-team kept chanting Taylor's two-four-six-eight rhyme.

I opened the deepest desk drawer and found about a gazillion burlap sacks tied with red string.

Gold. Tons of it. I reached for the top sack, thinking I could open it up for a peek.

"What the heck are you doing?" Hillyard whispered.

Petunia! Leave the gold alone and get on with it.

"Okay, okay," I whispered. I closed the gold drawer and tried the top drawer, and there it was: a brown leather book, about four by five inches, with gold writing on the cover. I picked it up, but—"Jeez'm!"—I threw it down because it was *warm*, in this creepy, human, throbby way that was scary and gross at the same time.

"You dropped it," Hillyard said.

"It's alive!"

"Nah." Hillyard picked it up and whispered, "Yish!" and handed it off to me like it was a hot potato. "It's got *circulation* or something."

This time I managed to hang on to the thing. The leather was soft and smooth, like Annabelle's old wallet on her dresser. But pulsing. Gross.

Open it, Petunia. The word you're looking for is "transformatio," transformation. It's Latin. STAY SILENT.

Vilma's handwriting was almost impossible to make out. She used some thick, scratchy pen—maybe even a quill—with black ink that smudged a lot and sometimes faded to light gray. The letters were packed in close together, hardly a space in between, and the paper was so thin the ink bled through in places. Sometimes she wrote sideways on the margin and upside down across the top and bottom.

I flipped page after page after page. This was impossible.

The thumping stopped outside, but now there was a siren. I was only about a quarter of the way through the book. Hillyard rushed out, then back in. "We gotta go. The B-teamers ran away. Vilma'll be in here any minute."

Give it up, Petunia. Being a chicken isn't so bad. A short life, but not an unpleasant one.

"Couple more pages," I muttered. The book hummed louder, got hotter. Pages flipped out of my fingers like there was a high wind. I kept leafing through the best I could, looking, looking, except what I was really seeing was Rachel dumping orange soda on Taylor, Rachel sitting with me after Annabelle died, and now she was a chicken because of me.

Petunia! Close that book and get out of there! DO NOT SPEAK AGAIN.

Hillyard jiggled my elbow. "C'mon. We gotta go."

The book throbbed at me, gold letters pulsing on the front cover. Before I knew it, my mouth opened all by itself, and I heard myself read those gold letters right out loud: "*Liber Vilmae Bliksemae.*"

Petuniaaaa, Margily moaned. *You said her naaaame.*

Screeeeee . . . The book squealed, ten times shriller than the police siren outside. I dropped it and we turned to run, but Vilma burst through the doorway, red and roaring, a froth of spit around her mouth that I would have thought was disgusting if I wasn't freaking out so bad. She grabbed at Hillyard's arm and he shrieked and managed to twist away from her and he hollered, "Run!" and so we did, out of the room and through the living room and the kitchen and out the door, pelted for the steps to my house. My floppy sandal came right off but I didn't even stop for that.

Oh Petunia. Oh no, Petunia. My dear child, I have no choice.

Vilma was shrieking behind us but then her voice slowed down, chanting. The air went thick, humid.

We barreled through my back door, not worrying about waking anybody up, and ran around locking doors and windows and into my room, where we huddled, the two of us, on the floor.

Something bellowed, right overhead, worse than anything we heard from Vilma.

Whump-whump-whump. Close by.

"Is that Margily?" Hillyard whispered.

Bang! Thunder clapped overhead like the end of the world. Wind came up, screaming like it wanted to carry us to Oz. We hunkered down, hands over our heads. The house rattled and creaked and moaned and maybe it was going to fall down on us.

Joy, Margily said.

"Are you kidding me?" I yelled.

The wind was like a freight train—louder than that, even—louder, louder, and it went on and on until I couldn't, *couldn't* stand another minute.

A crash outside, a thud I felt in my gut.

Then silence.

Like our ears were stuffed with cotton.

"Hope the B-team is all right." Hillyard's voice was shaking.

"Margily?" I whispered. No answer.

Mim and Janice were moving around upstairs, calling to each other. Mim yelled down the stairs, "Donna? You okay? That was a monster!"

She didn't know the half of it.

"I'm fine!" I yelled. We sat up and looked around. Ursa Major shone on the ceiling, undamaged. The floor was right there under us.

"I better get home," Hillyard whispered. "What if my mom checks on me?"

I led him out to the back deck. He switched on his headlamp. Which was when we saw all the branches.

And leaves, wet and shining. I turned my headlamp on too. Something massive filled the backyard. I went hollow like a cheap chocolate bunny.

Our big maple was down, the workshop squashed flat under all those branches. The truck would be flattened too. "Annabelle," I whispered, because she loved that truck.

"Oh, man," Hillyard said. "My dad was going to buy those tools."

I thought about Mim and Annabelle teaching me the lathe and how I made the drawer knob and now I would never know what I could've done to make it not wonky-looking.

It was like a river swooshed into my brain and washed half of it away.

Margily. How could she do this to me?

"Donna?" Mim's voice, in my room. "Where are you?"

Hillyard melted off into the darkness. Mim switched on the deck light and came out, and she saw the tree.

"This is my fault," I said. "I made Ms. Bliksem turn Rachel and her aunt Dana into chickens and I looked at Ms. Bliksem's book and everybody said I should leave but I didn't, and I said the words and she got mad and rode her dragon to make a thunderstorm."

Mim sat down on a deck chair, getting her butt all wet but she didn't seem to care. She shuddered like she was starting to cry but stifling it. Mim never cried.

"We needed to sell that stuff," was all she said.

"This is my fault," I said again.

"I don't need fantasies right now, Donna." She rubbed her face with her hands. "We should have moved away months ago. I'm starting to hate this place . . . this *river*."

Janice turned on the light in the kitchen. I left Mim out there staring into the dark. "I did this," I said, and I told Janice about Rachel, the chickens, Mr. Altin, the book—everything.

She sat down, in shock like she got a C on something. Finally she said, "Stay away from that old woman. And the dragon."

Well, duh, because I was pretty sure I didn't have a cleaning job anymore. But I went ahead and said, "If I do that, no more gold." I think I wanted her to tell me I was worth more than money. Like we were in this together, no matter what.

Janice shoved back her chair and stood up. "True. But if you get hurt we'll have to pay some doctor to fix you." She walked to the living room door, turned around. "Unless she offs you. That would be cheaper." Her eyes were cold as cold, cold, cold. "And in case you're wondering, this *is* your fault."

She was gone.

I was definitely going to Cousin Betty's. We might lose the house.

And Rachel was still a chicken.

CHAPTER FIFTEEN

Bad Luck Day

I slept for, like, an hour that night. It was too hard to think about Cousin Betty and losing the house, so instead I tried to think how to rescue Rachel.

I could tell Mim, but what could she do? Call the police? What could *they* do?

Anyways, who'd believe any of it?

Petunia, I'm so sorry.

"Don't call me that."

I did tell you to drop the book and run.

"Leave me alone." Last thing I needed was somebody else telling me this was all my fault. Especially when she just destroyed my life.

As you wish.

I could feel it when she left me—like somebody opened a door in my head and let the cold in. I never felt so alone in my life. Which I deserved. I kept imagining Rachel, huddled with the other chickens, maybe starting to peck for bugs like a real hen.

I needed that little leather book. But Vilma would never let it out of her sight now.

The next day, Wednesday, I woke up with Florinda the My Little Pony clutched in my hand so tight she left marks.

At breakfast, I could tell Mim didn't sleep much either—her face was all puffy. Janice sat at the table eating her yogurt without even once clicking the spoon against her tongue stud. That was how weird everything was.

I needed to find out if Rachel was still Rachel so I left for school early, walking along the river to Hillyard's instead of going up the steps to Vilma's. Hillyard ran out when I got to his place, and we headed to the pixie/ghost house.

Which wasn't a house anymore, at least not inside.

It was a barnyard.

We walked in the kitchen door and the B-team was standing there, mouths open. The floor was packed dirt and there were boxes with straw in them and a galvanized feeding gizmo with all these food pellets in it. The three original chickens were all scratching at the floor, eating the bugs they dug up—so obviously they forgot who they were.

"Who got all this stuff?" Mei Xing asked. "Sarah?"

Sarah shook her head. "Not me."

Flowers drifted down from the ceiling like pink snowflakes.

"Ohhh," Taylor breathed. "Pixies. They did it."

The Rachel-hen ran over, squawking, and stamped her foot at us, so that was a relief. But then she pecked at the dirt and came up with a bug.

Which she ate.

"Did you see that?" Hillyard looked horrified.

Taylor squatted down and shook her finger at Rachel's beak. "Don't *do* stuff like that. You have to hang in there till we figure out what to do."

"If the pixies could make a barnyard," Mei Xing said, "think they can change Rachel back?"

Huh. Worth a try. "Um, hello?" I called out. "Uh, thanks for making the barnyard—it's amazing. But, um, these birds are supposed to be humans. Think you could, like, change them back?"

Something zipped by and we all turned to look. Something else zipped on the other side of us. Pretty soon things were zipping all over the place but we couldn't see a single one.

Four hens and a rooster turned purple.

Then orange.

Then turquoise paisley. Mr. Pelletier too.

Rachel saw her reflection in the oven window, made a crooning sound. Guess she liked the paisley.

Somebody giggled, up by the ceiling.

If I might weigh in here.

"We don't need your help, Margily."

Petu—Donna. Again, let me apologize—

"I don't want to hear it. So can the pixies help or not?"

I'm afraid pixie magic is nowhere near complex enough to help. Nor is it, er, under control.

The feeding gizmo made a popping noise and turned into a huge blue overstuffed cushion, which exploded in a blizzard of white down.

"Noooooo." Mei Xing plunked herself down on the dirt floor. Even Taylor looked like she might cry.

Rachel preened her paisley feathers.

"We have to go to school," Sarah said. "If we don't show up everybody will think we disappeared."

"I'm sure we'll think of something," Hillyard said.

Dear children, please be careful. This day may prove a trifle . . . unpredictable.

Oh, great.

We took the Main Street route to school instead of going by Vilma's. Halfway there, we figured out what Margily meant by "unpredictable."

Hillyard was explaining to us that eating honey was stealing from bees unless you thanked them, which for some reason was calming me down, but then my backpack straps broke and the pack crashed to the sidewalk and my stuff fell out and rolled into the road.

Every pen I owned got smooshed. My math workbook drove away plastered to some guy's windshield, getting ripped and crumpled when he turned on his wipers to get the pages off. I barely rescued Florinda the My Little Pony from total squish-itude.

We ran around picking everything up and cars were honking and screeching their brakes and it was a real scene. Everybody except me was having a good time and laughing, but then everybody else's straps broke too and their packs crashed down and Hillyard's thermos rolled under an oil truck, which stove it up beyond all recognition. Mei Xing and Sarah got their cell phone screens cracked and Taylor's bottle of sun tea broke all over everything in her pack.

The rest of the way to school, we clutched our stupid packs to our chests because the straps were useless. We were super late.

While we waited in the office for the principal to get off the phone, Taylor whispered, "Hey, why was Margily apologizing?"

"Vilma made a thunderstorm destroy Donna's shed

and their truck," Hillyard whispered back. "Plus the tools my dad was going to buy."

Sarah got all wide-eyed. "And Margily . . . helped?"

I nodded. My throat hurt the way it does when you're going to cry.

"Wow," Mei Xing said. "Wasn't she sort of your friend?"

I nodded again.

"Some friend," Taylor said.

The principal came out and asked Mrs. Herrick if she'd heard anything from Rachel's aunt. They both looked really worried. Taylor shot me a look, and I could see she was thinking the same thing I was: We needed to think of some excuse for Rachel, didn't we? I imagined the police trying to talk to Vilma and getting turned into even more chickens.

We all got recess detention for being late, and when I got to my locker, it wouldn't open. I tried the combination again. Still wouldn't open. "Huh. My locker won't—"

"Hey." Hillyard rattled his locker at the end of the hall. "Did they change our combinations or something?"

Mei Xing kicked her locker a couple times, but that didn't work either. We had to get the custodian to come and break the lockers open.

We walked into language arts in time for a surprise

quiz on synonyms and antonyms. Here's a synonym for how the day was going so far: Jeez'm crow.

In gym class, Hillyard tripped and fell face-first into the miniature swamp behind third base, which nobody ever saw happen before except in a cartoon. With no Rachel to braid her hair, Taylor got a hunk of it caught in the chain on a swing and had to have it cut off.

Our new locker combinations didn't work either. The custodian took the locks out completely and taped the doors shut.

At lunchtime, Taylor thought to sneak into the computer room and send an email to the school from Johnson's Food Mart—Margily got the password out of some guy's head who worked for Aunt Dana. The email said Dana took Rachel to meet her parents in Cincinnati because of a family emergency.

So *that* was okay. But ten minutes later all five of us dropped our trays in the lunchroom. Spaghetti and peas. All at the same time, so the teachers thought we did it on purpose. We got two more recess detentions.

This was all before two o'clock. At 2:05, Hillyard's dad came to get him because his mom slipped and fell down their back steps and broke her thumb.

The *look* Hillyard gave me as he packed up to leave.

And it hit the rest of us: What did Vilma do to *our* parents? We waited until three, telling each other somebody would call us if something was wrong. Soon as the bell rang, we all blasted out of school and ran home.

Janice was in the kitchen, drinking milk straight out of the carton, when I burst through the door. "Where's Mim?" I panted.

"At work. What've you done now?" Cold, cold, cold.

"Hillyard's mother broke her thumb."

"Oh yeah?"

"She fell down the back steps." Pacing, pacing. It was three twenty. Earliest Mim ever got home was five.

"So you think it was Vilma?"

"Don't you?"

Janice took a deep, calming breath. "I'm not prepared to freak out about something this unscientific."

"The dragon and Vilma make thunderstorms. They wrecked our shop and killed our truck. I had a terrible bad luck day and so did Hillyard and so did thirty-three-point-three percent of the basketball B-team. My ex–best friend is a hen. Hillyard's mother got hurt. And you think it's unscientific to *worry*?"

"You may have a point."

Which Mim proved that exact minute by bursting through the door super early, throwing her briefcase across the kitchen, and stomping up the stairs.

Her bedroom door slammed.

"That's ominous," Janice said.

I put Mim's briefcase on the windowsill where she usually stashed it. Janice made like she was wiping the counter with a sponge, but she kept wiping the same part over and over. "Somebody should go up there," she said.

"You're the oldest."

"You're Little Miss Reliable."

"Not anymore."

Janice threw her sponge in the sink and went for the door, grabbing me by the sleeve. "We'll both go."

So we went up there together, which you could get all heart-warmed about except of course it was only temporary.

We didn't knock on Mim's door—barged in before we had a chance to think about it. Mim was facedown on her bed with her shoes on, even though her bedspread is white and her grammy crocheted it.

"Not now, girls," she said, muffled.

"No chance," said Janice. "We have a right to know what's going on."

"We love you, Mim," I said.

Janice muttered something that sounded like "Miss Reliable."

At last, Mim swung her legs over the side of the bed to face us, except she looked at her shoes instead of us.

She wiped the tears and mascara streaks off her face with the tail of her shirt.

"I lost my job," she said.

We stared at her like she turned bright green. I mean, the woman is the perfect employee. She doesn't even take sick days. Plus, she knows her stuff.

"How . . . ?" Janice croaked.

"Layoffs. Too many supervisors at my pay grade."

"Is it forever?" My voice was even croakier than Janice's.

Mim examined her right foot like she wanted to buy it. "If there's an opening someplace on campus I can try for it. But this job, my job—it's gone."

We watched her look at her foot. Janice said, "Are we going to lose the house?"

Well, that got Mim to look up. She glared at Janice. "No!"

"Really? Why not?"

Mim stood up. "Because I won't let it happen, that's why." She pulled her sweater down over her hips, pushed up her sleeves over her elbows, straightened her shoulders. "Don't you worry, girlie-cues. I'll figure this out." She went downstairs to do data entry.

Janice broke the silence. "She'll have to sell a kidney."

"People buy kidneys?"

"Don't even think about it, Miss Reliable."

I stored the idea away, just in case. "She'll get another job."

"Dream on, Petunia." Janice headed for the door. "Hope you weren't planning to go to college."

"I wasn't."

"Lucky you."

"Thought you weren't either."

She went in her room and shut the door.

Downstairs, Mim was at the kitchen table, tap-tap-tapping, her mouth a dark line like an angry Muppet.

I almost made it to my room when she said, "It's not easy being a woman in a carpentry department. You know that? Nobody cuts you a break. Not one."

What do you say to that? "We're really proud of you, Mim."

"Only reason I made it, it's because I'm tough. Cousin Betty toughened me up at the age of eight. Remember that."

Wouldn't you know it, right then her computer chimed with a video call. Cousin Betty, had to be. Mim said, "Come say hello to her."

"I have a math test tomorrow. Gotta study."

"This won't take a minute."

"Hi there, dearie," Betty said when I went to stand behind Mim. "School almost over?"

"No," I said.

"That's okay. Soon." She turned away from the screen and yelled into the kitchen behind her, "Anthony! Andrew! Don't you dare shave that dog again!" She turned back. "Fur'll grow, I guess. Into everything, those two."

Mim opened her mouth, shut it again.

"Listen, Nancy Jane, I got the best idea. You'll love it. Our neighbors're going away for a whole year, starting first of July. She got transferred someplace overseas and his work's portable, so the whole family's going."

"That's nice," Mim said. What did this have to do with us?

"It's great! The house'll be empty and they need a good house sitter."

Mim shook her head. "Donna's way too young to do something like that."

"Not Donna, silly. The whole bunch of you! You could come live here and rent out your house, make some money. This is your chance to get ahead!"

Mim was, like, frozen. Me too.

"But . . ." Mim stopped to swallow. "But . . . my job." Which was a surprising thing to say because . . . well, you know why.

"Oh, that job's nothing special. You can get three of 'em like that down here. And you'll be right next door to me! You need somebody to take care of you now that Annabelle's gone."

Mim's back straightened. "We don't need anybody to take care of us."

"Oh, dearie." Cousin Betty laughed her brittle, *hee-hee-hee* laugh. "You're all work and no housework, always have been."

"*I* do the housework," I said.

"Well, dearie, you come right down and do it here."

Mim was silent and so was I.

"Chances like this don't come along every day," Cousin Betty said.

"We'll think about it," Mim said. "Gotta go now."

Just as Mim hit the disconnect button, Cousin Betty screamed, "Anthony! Is that my good curling iron?" And she was gone. I did not want to know what the Evil Boy Twins were doing with a curling iron.

Mim sat there, her hand still on the laptop's touch pad. "Mim?" I said.

"I love my job." She sounded surprised. "Loved it."

"It was a *desk* job," I said. "Now you can go back to being a carpenter like you're supposed to. Like Annabelle said—"

"Annabelle, puh." It was kind of a laugh but not like Mim thought anything was so funny. "I loved that job.

I don't know why Annabelle thought working with your hands is so much nobler than sitting at a desk."

I felt like the world shifted. "But . . . but you're not . . . banging nails or . . . *anything*."

"There's nothing wrong with banging nails. But I'm the *boss*, Girlie-cue. I make the plans and order the materials and come up with the schedule and organize the crew. I love that. It's . . . it's like putting a jigsaw puzzle together. Making order out of chaos. It's what I was born to do."

"But . . . but you and Annabelle . . ."

My face must've been, like, this big mass of misery, because she took my hands in hers. "I love banging nails too, Girlie-cue. Someday maybe I'll have time to do that on the weekends, for fun. We could build something together again, you and me." She squeezed my hands. "I'm still so proud of the way you helped us build the workshop. I think about that all the time."

"You do?"

"I do. But I need to get some kind of job, don't I?" She went back to her laptop, hitting a key to wake up the screen. "Betty's not dumb. I'll give her that."

"Mim, *please* don't make us go live with Cousin Betty."

She didn't look up. "Better all of us than only you, right?"

"Better none of us."

She pressed her lips together, already tap-tap-tapping on her keyboard. "Maybe we need to start over—get away for a little while, from this house and *especially* from that river. Go do your homework, Donna."

In my room, I got out my math, but it was hard to concentrate when the world was ending.

Rachel was a chicken, maybe forever. Mim lost her job. The truck and the shed were gone. We were probably moving next door to Cousin Betty and the Evil Boy Twins. And it was all my fault.

I closed my eyes and remembered back to last August, when Annabelle was still here. She made dinner every night, fixed anything that broke, helped me on the lathe. Janice was always quoting Shakespeare. Mim laughed sometimes, and they polished the big red truck till it sparkled like a ruby. Annabelle went to check on Mrs. Wittingham every day, and almost always came home with cookies or lasagna for the freezer.

Cousin Betty was some relative I barely knew.

Dragons were fairy tales.

CHAPTER SIXTEEN

Option to Buy

At recess the next day, me and Hillyard and the B-team did one of our detentions. The B-team had to help the cook clean the refrigerator. Hillyard and I had to clean the grease trap in the kitchen. We smelled like an ancient fryolator the whole rest of the day.

Hillyard looked like a ghost. Guess he didn't sleep much, feeling guilty about his mom's broken thumb.

We went to see Rachel after school, which was totally depressing. Rachel was a two-day-old chicken now, so we only had two more days to figure out how to save her, maybe three. Margily told us that Vilma kept her book on her all the time now. Nobody could think of a way to take it away from her.

Rachel kept scratching at the dirt like a chicken looking for bugs. We sat on the floor and talked to her, hoping that would make her human side stick around longer. It was all we could think of to do.

Taylor told the "pig-breath" story from the sleepover I wasn't invited to. That was cold, reminding me about that sleepover. But the story was a big hit. Rachel did seem to be listening—turns out chickens can laugh, though it sounds like clucking.

We decided we'd take turns staying with her, try to keep her human. Sarah would come over after supper, when her dad would be working in his office. I'd come over after Mim and Janice went to bed because I was so good at sneaking out now. The next day, Friday, Taylor and Mei Xing would fake being sick and take turns sneaking over while their parents were at work.

Meanwhile, we'd think, think, think.

Hillyard and I walked to his house together, and I went on to mine, walking along the river. Couldn't help watching for a green spike to surface.

I'm here, Petunia. You are doing the right thing with your friend.

"Don't call me that. I don't care where you are."

She didn't say anything but I knew she was still there. "If you're going to hang around, the least you could do is tell me what else we can do for Rachel. I mean—"

But that was when the breath got knocked right out of me.

A "For Rent" sign, at the end of our driveway. With a big green sticker that said, "Option to Buy."

I lit out for the house like a bear was after me. Upstairs, the folding steps to the attic were pulled down from the ceiling and Mim was hauling a box of our old toys into her bedroom.

"Hi, Girlie-cue," she said, like the sun was shining and she drank too much coffee. "Real estate agent says we'll rent this place in a heartbeat, so we better start packing and throwing things out. Go through this box and see what you want to keep, okay?" She opened another box marked "Christmas."

"Mim. Option to *buy?*"

She straightened up. "Oh, the agent put that on. It doesn't mean we *have* to sell it. Best to have choices, she says."

I stood there like I had no brain at all, which I didn't. Mim pulled out this annoying burping Santa that Annabelle bought when I was five, tossed it in another box marked "swap shop."

I grabbed her arm. "Mim. We *can't*. I mean, this is our *home*. Annabelle. The river."

"Girlie-cue." She patted my hand. "Betty had a point. This'll help us get back on our feet. Get strong again. It's time to take action."

"But we'd be living next door to Cousin Betty."

Mim plugged in some Christmas tree lights to see if

they worked. "We won't be there forever. Just till the finances settle down." She looked out the window at the river. "Maybe we'll come back here. Maybe we won't."

I went downstairs and stood in the kitchen, eyeballing the fallen tree outside the window.

Janice walked in from outside and grabbed her backpack. "I'm eating at Michelle's."

"Good. More peanut butter for me and Mim."

"So," she said, "guess you're gonna be next door to Cousin Betty."

"Won't be just me. You'll be there too."

She slung her pack on her back. "Nope. I'm staying here."

"What?"

"Michelle's parents say I can live with them till I graduate."

"Mim'll never let you do that."

"I'm sixteen. I can be emancipated."

"You can be what?"

"I can be emancipated. Freed. I can legally be on my own."

I couldn't stand up and think at the same time, so I sat down at the table.

Janice stood there by the door. "Nothing to say?"

"You . . . you're my *sister*."

She had no expression on her face. "Yeah, well. We're

not exactly best buds, are we?" She looked like she was going to say something more. But she didn't.

She went out and slammed the door behind her.

How could we be like we were last August and now we were like this?

I had to be careful sneaking out that night to sit with Rachel—Vilma was in the woods next door with a flashlight, making clucking noises. Like those chickens would ever come near her.

In the pixie kitchen, stroking Rachel's feathery head with one finger, I kept thinking about when we were real little and how we spit-swore to be friends forever and Annabelle called us The Inseparables. In the summer we used to sleep over at each other's house a couple or three times a week.

But, you know, sometimes remembering the good times doesn't make you feel all that good. Like, say, if a thunder mage just destroyed your whole life. And your Annabelle is gone and you're moving away from your river to a place with leeches and Evil Boy Twins.

And your best friend got turned into a chicken.

I was so sick of all this.

"You know what, Rachel? We probably have to move. And instead of doing all the cooking and cleaning just at my house like . . . like Cinderella, I'll have to do it at

Cousin Betty's too, because she'll be next door with her nasty little boys. But me and you, we're not friends anymore so probably you don't care and I don't know why I'm even telling you this and I am *so tired* of being me."

Rachel butted her head against my arm.

I closed my eyes and leaned my head back against the wall. "Nothing's been right since Annabelle died." Rachel snuggled down next to me and crooned. It came to me that this was the first time in months I told anyone what I was feeling. It felt good.

I put my arm around the little hen, gently. "You were great that day she died," I whispered. Rachel snuggled even closer.

The next day after school, I threw every one of my old toys in the "swap shop" box. I went in my room and got Raggedy Ann and Andy and threw them in there. They hardly had faces left, I used to cuddle them so hard. My stuffed animals went too. Like Mim said, time to get strong.

I kept Florinda the My Little Pony. She was grimy. Who'd want her.

I stuck her back under my pillow.

Mim made me help pack up the files from her desk in her room, and when she went downstairs to do data entry, I kept going, and let me tell you it wasn't any picnic. I had to pack a green folder full of mortgage letters, and a blue one with stuff about the truck loan.

Then a yellow one marked "Annabelle," which I opened and wasn't *that* a kick in the pants.

First thing I saw was a letter to Mim in Annabelle's writing—her loopy cursive, which about killed me to see. It must've been from when my dad left, right before I was born and not long before she moved in with Mim to help out.

This isn't your fault, Annabelle wrote. *I know you're grieving but you don't have to deal with everything alone. Don't retreat into yourself the way you always do. Let other people help (me, for example). Talk to people. You've always wanted to be a mom, so let your little girls into your heart, let them see who you really are. You don't have to be perfect.*

There was a lot of other stuff about exercising and eating right and allowing herself to be sad. It must've been so tough for Mim. No picnic for Janice, either—she was old enough to know Dad was gone. Janice never talked about it, at least not with me. Maybe she did with Annabelle.

Underneath the letter were the four missing pages from Annabelle's Guide. I knew because they were typed with holes punched in the side and numbered 115 to 118. A note was paper-clipped to the pages in Mim's straight-up-and-down printing: *Sorry, sister. I love you,* dated a week after Annabelle died, one day after I got my first recipe out of the Guide.

I started reading.

I was twelve and Nancy Jane was five, Annabelle wrote, *when a pixie let us see him.*

What.

We were living upriver back then. It was summertime and a full moon, and we were too hungry to sleep. We were on the porch and I was telling her about the man in the moon when these little glowing things—too big for fireflies—started flitting all over the woods. I blinked, and there was this tiny guy, maybe two inches tall, standing on the railing in front of us, raggedy and with blue tattoos all over, holding a flaming torch. He grinned at us, waved, and zipped away, too fast to see.

Pixies were real. Jeez'm crow.

I started leaving candy out for them, in a little dish with a cover, and I did that until my last day at home. Once in a while they left a pink flower for me. Donna and I put candy out now, in Nancy Jane's little houses beside the river. Donna thinks it's a game but I found pink flowers all over my veggie garden one morning, and I'm darn sure they protect it. No slugs, and I don't even bother fencing it from deer and raccoons and hares. The neighbors can't believe it.

They turned the tomatoes into walnuts this year,

*which wasn't so great, but that only lasted a couple
of days.*

*Nancy Jane swears we never saw that pixie, says I
was dreaming. But I know I wasn't. I've talked to older
people in town and they told me what they know. I've
tried to reproduce their knowledge here. Nan doesn't like
me to talk about it to the kids. But they hardly ever look
in the Guide and neither does she, so I think I'm safe
putting this here. Maybe someday they'll see it.*

"Annabelle," I whispered. I never wanted to talk to
anybody so much in my entire life. I wanted to tell her
the pixies were still around, and they were helping me
because of those candy bars and the water in the basins.

The rest of what Annabelle wrote was all about ley
lines and the pixies' simple magic and how they lived
their lives, stuff Margily already told us. She said pixies
have no use for magic rings or toadstools or wands—
their magic is all in themselves, as long as there's a river
nearby. *That seems smart*, Annabelle wrote. *I never liked
stories about magic stored in some object another person could use
or destroy. Made no sense to me. Better to rely on yourself and
your fellow creatures, I always thought.*

Annabelle knew about pixies. And Mim knew but
wouldn't admit it. And she hid pages from the Guide!

I took the pages downstairs, thinking I'd maybe confront Mim with them, but when I walked into the kitchen she had her head in her hands. So I didn't say anything. Instead, I went in Annabelle's room and grabbed a pair of her socks, gold with silver toes and heels. I stuck them in my pocket. Felt like I needed her with me right now, you know?

Saturday, a week after we started working on Vilma's shed, the real estate lady brought, like, half a dozen people to look at our house and they wouldn't shut up about how adorable it was.

"You girls better start packing up your rooms," Mim said that night while I boiled the water for the macaroni. "This could move faster than we think." She ran back up to get more junk out of the attic before supper. Janice didn't tell Mim yet about being emaciated, or whatever she called it. She left for Michelle's again, which was good because I couldn't even look at her.

I couldn't look at Mim, either, because I wanted *so bad* to holler at her about Annabelle and the pixies and I knew I shouldn't. So basically I was looking at no one.

After supper, Mim packed some more and went to bed early. I went out on the porch to smell the river. And, hey, maybe see a pixie.

The river, my river, glistened in cloudy moonlight.

Good evening, Donna. It's terrible that you might be moving away.

I almost said to leave me the heck alone, she'd done enough damage. But I had to tell someone. "Annabelle knew about pixies."

Doesn't surprise me in the least.

"Where are you now?"

To your north with Madame Vilma. Making a storm for no apparent reason except our entertainment.

I closed my eyes to imagine what Margily was seeing right now, the Maine woods spread out below her in a rush of air. Instead, weirdly, I saw a drawer full of burlap bags. Full of gold. In an empty house.

Out of nowhere, I felt a rush of yearning. And then hope. "Exactly how far away are you, Margily?" I whispered.

Donna. I don't like what I'm seeing in your mind.

"Mim says we need to take action."

There is no possible action to take involving Madame Vilma's gold.

It wouldn't be stealing, not really. Not after what Vilma did to us. She owed us.

The only time Rachel and me stole something—candy bars, of course—Annabelle marched us back to return them in front of everybody, and it was so humiliating both of us cried till we were out of breath.

One bag, though. That was all we'd need to pay off

the loans and tide us over till Mim got another job. Vilma'd never even notice.

Maybe Mim wouldn't *need* a new job. She could start her own business, doing all the planning and stuff she said she loved.

Petun—Donna. Dear. Go to bed.

A rumble of thunder, sounding far, far away.

Two minutes later, I was in my room putting on a navy-blue long-sleeved T-shirt and my darkest jeans. I grabbed gloves, so I wouldn't leave fingerprints. (Pretty smart, don't you think?) Unfortunately, the only gloves I could find were Annabelle's polka-dot gardening gloves.

I stuck Annabelle's gold socks in my pocket, even though she would've hated what I was doing.

"She'd understand," I whispered as I let myself out the back door, super quiet, and snuck over to the hillside steps like some little night creature.

Petunia. Stop this. You don't know what you're doing.

"Stop calling me Petunia."

The back door was locked. So was the front. But here's the thing about houses with outside cellar doors: Nobody ever thinks to lock them. Sure enough, Vilma's was open. I slipped into the cellar—good thing I brought a flashlight—and crept upstairs.

Donna, I feel we haven't really talked about this gold.

I stopped at the head of the stairs. "Why do we need to talk about it?"

This gold is not . . . normal.

"Looked perfectly normal to me." So shiny, so pure.

It's not. It's mage gold, jolted to life by lightning, created for greedy kings. Touching it has unfortunate effects.

"Like what?" Didn't do anything to me.

So shiny.

Any gold can incite madness, but this is more like possession. Especially in large quantity, and especially if you steal it, greed responding to greed. This gold knows what it's doing. Keep it by you long enough and it will never let you go. Look at Madame Vilma—when she left her sister, she was incapable of leaving that gold behind. And she didn't just take her share—she took it all.

I remembered what Vilma said to Mr. Altin: *It is freely given. It will not harm you.*

That was a lie. Mage gold does lose its curse if it is freely given, but that happens only if the giver expects nothing for herself in return. Madame Vilma exchanged that gold for currency—not freely given at all. Your little coin was exchanged for your service, also not given freely. One coin, kept only for a day—I hoped it wouldn't be enough to harm you. But here you are, craving more of it.

Didn't harm me at all. *I* wasn't greedy.

Donna. I beg you. Go home.

I ignored her. One minute later I was standing in Vilma's spare bedroom, my light jigging around because my hands were shaking. Two pairs of eyes shone back at me from the top of the desk, which freaked me out so bad I almost shrieked. They turned out to be on a brand-new pair of furry bedroom slippers with raccoon ears.

Okay, they were strange. But not why I was here. My light found the bottom desk drawer.

Would the gold scream, like the magic book? Holding my breath, I eased the drawer open and there were the burlap bags.

Here goes nothing, I thought. I reached into the drawer, grabbed a bag. It was heavier than I expected and I stumbled a little. The house remained silent. My fingers were still attached to my hand. I seemed to be human.

I plumped up the other bags in the drawer, hoping you couldn't tell one was missing. A minute later I was out through the cellar, down the hillside steps and into the kitchen, where I stood against the door, breathing hard, a burlap bag of gold clutched to my chest.

The gold made a happy, purring sound.

CHAPTER SEVENTEEN

Possession

I did it. I felt wonderful. You'd think I'd feel like a sneak and a thief and a traitor. But no. A whole new world opened up before me, a world without loans, where Mim didn't have to work so hard and we could build a tree house or something together and Janice wasn't a grump-head.

Rescuing Rachel wasn't part of the picture. I hadn't thought about her for hours, forgot all about sitting with her to keep her human. The only thing on my mind was this gold, purring in my hand.

A car door slammed outside. Janice, home earlier than I expected. I booked it for my room, changed my mind, booked it for Annabelle's because . . . I dunno. It seemed like a safer place to hide things.

I was standing in front of Annabelle's bureau, trying to choose a drawer, when the door opened behind me. "I came home," Janice said. "What's that in your hand?"

I whipped the bag of gold out of sight behind my back. "Nothing."

Janice took three strides and grabbed the bag out of my hand before I could even move. Like me, she wasn't expecting it to be so heavy—she dropped it and coins spilled out on the floor.

We both stared down at the coins, delicate and glistening on Annabelle's big braided rug.

"That's gold," Janice said.

"Duh."

"She's forgiven you? And she's paying you a thousand bucks an hour?"

I opened my mouth. I shut my mouth. I dropped to my knees and scooped the coins back into their bag, fumbling a bit because of the gloves.

"Why are you wearing Annabelle's gardening gloves?" Janice peered into my face and her jaw dropped open. "Did you"—her voice dropped to a whisper—"did you *steal* this?"

"Shut up." I tied the bag closed and stood, clutching it, purring, to my chest. "Vilma owes us. She wrecked our truck and stuff."

"You kinda brought it on when you tried to steal her

book, but I see your point." She stood there, chewing her lip. Gave a decisive nod. "Right. We'll have to sell it. I'll get Michelle to drive us Monday after school. We'll find that other gold dealer, the one who isn't a rooster."

"We?"

She looked down her nose at me. "You're not the only one capable of taking action, you know."

"Why would you help? You don't care about me *or* Mim. You're leaving." I sounded whiney.

"I'm still part of this family. Anyway, if we cash in this gold you'll probably stay here and so will I."

"Big deal. Anytime things get tough, you go to Michelle's." Why couldn't I stop talking?

"So tell me, how would you deal with this without me and Michelle? You stole gold. Great. What's the next step?"

I had nothing to say.

"I thought so." She headed for the door, but paused before going out. "Good work, by the way."

I stuck the bag of gold behind Annabelle's sweaters in her bottom drawer. I took one coin out, though, so I could hold it in my hand and poke at it. I was sitting on my bed, gazing and poking, when Margily said, *Donna.*

"Now what?"

I regret to say, Madame Vilma has noticed her gold is missing. She's beginning a spell to track its location.

"*Track* it? You never said she could track it."

No, I didn't. I was too busy trying to stop you from doing this idiotic thing, prevent Madame Vilma from suspecting, and keep flying all at the same time.

I stood up.

She's only just begun to weave the spell. She's keeping it local because it's stronger that way and, frankly, she suspects you. If we hurry, I can get you and the gold out of range.

I headed for Annabelle's room to get the gold. "What do I do?"

Bring the gold down to the river. The gloves you wore too—they touched the gold. I'll put everything in my mouth—she can't track things there. Put that coin back in the bag with the others. Hurry!

Didn't have to tell me twice. Took me five minutes, tops, to get out the door with the gold and the gloves.

She's about to come see me! Hurry!

Margily was waiting for me at Table Rock. She opened her mouth, teeth glistening, spicy heat bathing my face, and I threw everything in. As I turned to run back to the house, a door slammed at Vilma's. No way I was going to make it home without her catching me.

"I'll hide," I whispered.

No, no, too dangerous. She'll sense your clothes—they'll have a whiff of gold on them too. Get on my back. Quick!

I was barely up there when Margily waded away from the rock, wings flapping. She went up steep as a roller coaster—we were through the clouds and into the moon-light in seconds. I clung to the spike in front of me, afraid I'd slip off backwards. She wheeled around and leveled off. *I'll take you upriver, to my home. It's far enough away.*

"You have a home?"

Such as it is. I dug it into the riverbank, above the rapids. It takes at least a century to make a true home.

"Jeez'm. How old are you?"

Can't really remember. Several hundred years. Madame Vilma is my third mage. The beat of her wings faltered. *Oof. She's summoning me. I'll have to drop you off and come back.*

She plunged into the darker world beneath the clouds—scary as heck—did her usual clumsy landing in the water, waded ashore, and knelt so I could slide onto the ground. We were two or three miles above the rapids, I figured.

We're too far away for her to track these now. Take them. She stuck out her tongue so I could grab the gold and the gloves, hot and spicy from her breath. *Stay here. I won't be long. I'll tell her I have a sore wing.*

She splashed back into the river, beat her wings, and took off, disappearing into the clouds in two seconds. I settled down under a tree.

The river smelled sweet, muddy, comforting. Some-thing rustled in the brush nearby. I hoped Margily would come back soon.

I picked up the bag of gold. It was heavy in my hand, full of riches, promises. Mr. Altin gave Vilma a four-inch stack of hundred-dollar bills for a bag this size. "This is mine," I said out loud. "I *need* it." Nobody could blame me for stealing it. I hugged it to my chest. It purred.

We'd find a gold dealer, far enough away so Vilma'd never track him down. Maybe Margily would fly us there in the night, with the gold in her mouth. I shut my eyes, imagining the moment when I handed Mim a four-inch stack of hundreds.

Whump, whump, whump . . . SPLASH. Margily was back. I could see her dark shape out on the water. She walked ashore and, to my surprise, knelt down to let someone slide off her back.

Janice.

She had a black trash bag in her hand. She flung it at me. "Yeah, so, this was a great idea, wasn't it?"

"What the heck . . . ?"

"The lizard barged into my head, told me to put some gold-free clothes together for you. She put up quite a fuss when I said I was coming too. Like I was going to let you go off somewhere in the dark with a bag of gold and a giant mythical beast."

Watch who you're calling mythical, evil girl. Sit down and don't either of you move an inch. My home is beneath you, and the entrance is underwater. I shall make a new entrance for you.

Another splash, and she was gone. Janice sat down next to me, hugged her knees. I hugged my stomach.

"I found another gold dealer," Janice said.

"Has to be pretty far away."

"He is."

"How far—?" I started to ask, but right then the earth shook so hard I almost fell over, something pounding from underneath.

Something broke through the dirt about ten feet away, waggled around.

Margily's tail, drilling a hole from underneath.

"Cripes!" Janice said. "Is she trying to kill us?"

Stay exactly where you are. I mean it.

"We are," I said. "We're right—"

The world exploded in bright white steam, blasting up through the hole with a roar like a movie monster. I shut my eyes and clapped my hands over my ears.

When it stopped, I opened my eyes, but they weren't used to the dark anymore so I couldn't see a thing. "Jeez'm, Margily. What the heck?

I had to smooth the sides of the hole. Find it and slide down. Be careful.

"*Find* it?" Janice said. "You just blinded us, you scaly—"

"Shut up, Janice." I got on my hands and knees and crawled, feeling with one hand, the bag of gold in the other. Janice dropped down next to me, so close our shoulders touched. Didn't take long to find the hole. We sat on the edge, dangling our feet. The soil was damp and crumbly, still hot, but it did feel like the sides were smooth. "We're going to be filthy," Janice muttered.

I was not real happy about sliding into a hole I couldn't see the bottom of. "Uh, Margily? Any way you can make a light?"

Of course. How silly of me. Here.

Light flickered below, showing us a chute slanting like a playground slide. We had to edge around to find the best angle. *I'd suggest you let it cool for a few minutes.*

"This is going to be gross," Janice said. "And I don't see how we're getting out, it's so mucky."

Then don't come down.

"Yeah, right. I'm not letting my sister out of my sight, lizard." I was almost flattered, but then she added: "We need her. She's a gold mine."

We waited, checking the heat of the soil now and then. At last Janice said she thought it wouldn't kill us.

Here goes, I thought. I dropped into the hole, hugging my bag of gold, and slid down the warm mud, landing on my butt in some soft stuff—a pile of dead marsh grass, it turned out. I hustled out of the way, and Janice plopped onto the grass behind me, hauling my bag of clothes behind her.

There were piles of dead grass all over the floor—something to lie on, I guessed. "Isn't grass kind of a fire hazard for somebody with hot breath?" I asked.

Flames won't hurt me. In fact, I rather like them. I will be careful with you two around, however.

She was sitting like a dog, her tail wrapped around her, in the middle of a ginormous glass cave, the walls studded with quartz stones—blue, pink, white, even green—flickering in the light of a burning pine knot stuck in the wall.

"Wow," I said.

Thank you. I did the best I could in a short time. Fortunately, the soil here is sandy and becomes glassy with intense heat. Bit sticky, until it hardened.

"Too bad that hole in the ground wasn't glass," Janice said. I had to admit, we were pretty muddy. "You could've said to bring a change of clothes for me too."

Nobody asked you to come in the first place. Now, Donna, give me the gold. I'll put it somewhere safe, you change your clothes, and I'll fly the two of you home before your mother notices you're gone.

"Um. Maybe I'll stay here." I found out I actually didn't *want* to give her the gold.

"Huh?" Janice said.

Don't be absurd. You can't stay here. Apart from your

mother's dismay, your absence will tell ᴄℳadame ᵛilma *exactly what happened. She has the power to make me tell where you are.*

My hand tightened on the gold. "What are you going to do with this? How do I know you won't fly off with it and I'll never see you again?" What was I saying?

"You're being an idiot. Give me that." Janice went to grab the gold out of my hand but I shoved her away from me, so hard she slipped on the glass floor and landed on her butt.

Oh dear. Margily's huge head swooped in close, her cobalt-blue eyes staring into mine. *Donna, you're such a nice child, I was sure you'd hold out longer. I'm afraid this gold has you utterly in its power.*

"Does not." I felt fine. I just didn't want some dragon taking off with my gold. Or some sister, either.

"What do you mean, 'in its power'?" Janice asked.

"Supposedly stealing this gold makes you possessed or greedy or something." I hugged the bag of gold to my chest.

"Uh-huh. And of course you don't have any such problem."

"No." I decided to kick her if she came at me again. "I don't.

The dragon's tail moved so fast I didn't have time to

think. It struck like a snake, knocked the bag of gold out of my hand. Janice caught it and tossed it to Margily, who put her foot on it. I lunged for her, thinking . . . I don't know what I was thinking. Her tail blocked my path.

Change your clothes, Donna dear. You'll feel better in the fresh air.

"No!" I yelled, trying to push her tail out of my way.

Oh, Petunia. The tail snaked around me, lifting me up and out the chute she'd made for us. I got dumped outside on the ground, and a second later the trash bag with my clothes was next to me. A second after that, Janice climbed out of the hole, boosted by the tail.

Get those clothes off you, dear, and put them in the bag. I'll find them later, after I take you home.

I crawled back towards the lighted hole, I guess thinking I'd slide back in, get my gold somehow. Janice grabbed my arm and something rumbled underground. Everything went dark.

"Hah," Janice said. "She blocked up the bottom of the hole. Boy, are you a piece of work."

Breathe, Petunia. It will help.

So I did breathe, sitting there in the dark listening to the rapids in the distance, holding Annabelle's gold socks in my hand while Janice pulled clothes out of the trash bag and threw them at me.

I kept the socks in my hand on the ride home. But all I could think about was the gold I left behind.

When I shut my eyes that night, Annabelle's socks under my pillow next to Florinda, I saw gold coins, stacks and stacks of them. I had to get back to Margily's cave, find a way in, get my gold. It was *mine*.

I finally went to sleep, but I dreamed I got the Midas touch and turned Janice into this golden statue, her face frozen forever in a despairing scream. I woke up before it was light, tangled in a sweaty bedsheet. I lay there, tracing Herbert with my finger, listening to the rapids.

Annabelle. What would she think of me now?

And without meaning to, I remembered Rachel, sitting with me all day after Annabelle died. Not trying to hug me, not making me talk . . . just there. For me.

Maybe Margily put that thought in my head. But it felt different. More like Annabelle—sweeter, somehow, more understanding but also a little bit stern.

The longer I lay there, tracing Herbert with my finger, the weirder it seemed that last night I deserted my friend for a bag of treasure, even if she did call me a loser.

I wanted that gold. I needed it. It was mine.

But I knew what I had to do.

CHAPTER EIGHTEEN

The Plan

Everybody was at the pixie house at the crack of dawn Sunday morning, even Janice. She said the situation was too dire to leave it to a bunch of snotty-nosed kids. It was cloudy and gloomy outside, matching my mood. I got, like, two hours of sleep.

When we walked in, Rachel was orange-and-green paisley. Mr. Altin the rooster was pink, Aunt Dana red and blue polka dot. The other two were bright green and silver. Mr. Pelletier was purple with red squiggles. At least the pixies were having a good time.

Rachel ate a worm, which pretty much freaked everybody out. She'd been a chicken for five days.

I was miserable. I needed my gold. I had come up with kind of a plan, though I sure was hoping somebody would think of something else.

"So," I said. "Any ideas for saving Rachel?" Sarah burst into tears. Guess that answered that.

Okay. All right. Okay. I had to do this.

I swallowed hard. "I stole a bag of Vilma's gold."

Well, that was a shocker. Sarah stopped crying and started hiccupping.

"Why the heck—" Hillyard started.

"Mim lost her job."

"Ohhhh." That was everybody except Janice. They knew we couldn't even afford cell phones.

"And we have to rent the house or sell it, and move away."

"Je-e-e-e-eze," Hillyard whispered.

"Yeah. But—I decided it's worse to be a chicken for life."

Rachel made a cooing sound and ran over to sit on my foot.

"So I was thinking, how about if I say I'll give it back if Vilma turns everybody human again?"

"Yay, Donna!" Mei Xing started clapping, then everybody did. I didn't know what to do with my face—I felt like a big fake since I was the one who got Rachel turned into a hen in the first place. Janice rolled her eyes.

Plus, now I had to tell Vilma I stole her gold.

Children, this is a commendable plan, but it won't work.

"Who you calling 'children'?" Janice said.

"Why won't it work?" asked Hillyard.

For the simple reason that Madame Vilma is thoroughly possessed by that gold and will not—cannot—be reliable. She will take it back and will not undo the transmogrifications.

"What do you mean, 'possessed by that gold'?" Sarah asked.

My face went all hot, remembering.

"Turns you into a gibbering idiot," Janice said helpfully.

To put it simply, the gold is cursed and makes you greedy unto madness if you keep it by you for long, especially if you steal it. Madame Vilma's family has been subject to this curse for generations.

I thought back to Mr. Altin's shop, how Vilma clung to her bag of gold like she didn't want it to leave her hands. I knew how she felt.

"Why isn't Donna possessed?" Mei Xing asked.

Janice snorted. I pretty much had to confess. "I am. Or I was . . ." I told them how Margily and Janice had to force me to leave the gold in her cave. "But . . . Rachel. And the others."

Donna has decided to give this gold up for her friend, expecting nothing for herself. That is redemption.

Hillyard frowned. "That's great, but how are we going to make sure Vilma doesn't take the gold without changing everybody back?"

Good question.

"Tie a string to it," Taylor suggested, "and pull it back if the birds don't change."

"She's pretty strong," I said. "I think she'll manage to hang on."

"Grab her book," Mei Xing said. But nobody wanted anything to do with that book, ever again.

"This is pitiful," Janice said.

"Oh yeah?" Taylor said. "What's your idea?" That shut my sister up.

I closed my eyes and tried to imagine what would happen. We'd be outside, that was for sure—no way I was going in that house. I'd hand her the gold first? Or she'd change the birds back and *then* I'd hand her the gold? I couldn't see how either one of those would work.

Except . . . what if we did both? "How about this— she gets some of the gold every time she changes some- body back. When the last bird turns human, she gets the last piece of gold."

Nobody could think of a better plan.

I'm still not sure she won't get the better of you, but this is the best— Margily's voice broke off. *Donna, did you by any chance keep an article of clothing from yesterday?*

"No," I said, but then I remembered. "I mean . . . yes. Um. Something in my pocket." I felt stupid saying it was a pair of socks.

Oh, PETUNIA. Man, she sounded ticked off. I let the

"Petunia" pass. *Madame Vilma is sensing something—she's not sure what. You must take action immediately.*

We all jumped up, panicky. I was going to have to do this *now*—in broad daylight. Walking through the neighborhood with polka-dot and paisley chickens to meet a dragon at the river. Oh, man.

"Bring the gold to Table Rock, Margily," I said.

Meaning no offense, Petunia, you should have companions with you when you touch that gold again. Best to have someone with you to make sure you, er, carry through with the plan.

"We'll all go," Sarah said.

"I want to meet the dragon anyways," said Taylor.

Mr. Pelletier was hard to catch, but Hillyard and Mei Xing finally managed it. Hillyard tied knots in his scarf (purple, gold, and royal blue today, with fringe) to make a Bizarro Bird carrier. The rest of us each grabbed a chicken and off we went, hoping the neighbors were still too sleepy to notice we had this colorful bunch of birds with us.

When we got to Table Rock, Margily was waiting for us underwater. We saw spikes at first, out in the middle of the river, then her beautiful green back, then—*splooooosh*—her gorgeous head rose up and up till it towered over us, all emerald-colored scales and cobalt-blue eyes.

Taylor sat down hard on the rock, Mr. Altin the rooster in her arms.

I crouched beside her. "You okay?"

She had tears in her eyes. "Dragons are real," she whispered.

Take the gold, Petunia, and rush it up to Vilma's before she begins to sense it. Put the gloves on first—maybe that'll slow the effect on you.

Margily opened her gigantic mouth, and there were the gloves and the gold. I handed Aunt Dana to Mei Xing, grabbed the gloves, waved them around to cool them off, and put them on. I took the gold. "Let's go!"

Be very careful, all of you. She is wily. Margily backed away from the rock and sank into the river.

When we made it up the hillside steps, Vilma was standing in her doorway, arms folded, eyes super-mad.

"You!" She pointed at me. "*You* stole my gold." Her face twisted up like an old apple. "We were family, I thought. You betray me *twice*—you meddle with my book, then you rob me."

"You can have the gold if you change everybody back into people." I discovered I was hugging the gold to my chest. It felt so right. I loved how it purred.

Rachel, I thought. Remember Rachel.

Vilma laughed the most evil laugh I ever heard. It wasn't, like, a cartoon evil-person laugh. It was like she really thought something was funny. "Do not move," she said, and hustled back into her house.

"What's she doing?" Hillyard whispered.

Petunia. Margily sounded, I dunno, upset. *Are you missing an article of clothing?*

Didn't have time to answer and didn't need to. Because Vilma came back out, her book in one hand and in the other . . .

A sandal. The stupid too-big sandal I lost the night I looked at her book.

Vilma smiled like the Grinch and started to chant. I yelled, because my hands were on fire.

A white feather sprouted from my wrist. Another. Another. I screamed and dropped the gold, stripped off the gloves to see tiny feathers all over my hands.

"Bring that bag to me, one of you," Vilma said.

I doubled over in agony. More feathers sprouted.

"You old witch!" Janice shoved past me and ran for Vilma.

"Janice," I gasped. "Don't let her touch you!"

"Come on!" Hillyard yelled. He and the B-team dropped their chickens and ran after Janice. But they were too late. Vilma leaped down from her back stoop, had Janice by the arm before she could knock the book away.

My hands stopped burning.

Janice screamed.

CHAPTER NINETEEN

Tears of a Stork

Janice heaved around and arched her back, let out a shriek that went through me like a knife. Sarah and Mei Xing were screaming and trying to pull Janice away, Hillyard and Taylor pounding on Vilma's back.

I rushed to Janice and tried to grab her hand but she shook me off. "Get Mim!" she yelled, and doubled over, panting.

I only made it halfway down the hillside steps—Mim was already climbing up, because I guess we were kinda loud. I turned and scuttled back up the steps just in time for Janice to scream and crumple to the ground under Vilma's hands.

Fireflies, swarming everywhere. Weird. I swatted one away from my face, then realized: Ohhhh. Pixies. But what could they do?

The tiny lights darted over to the chickens, whirled around them. Next thing I knew, all the birds launched themselves at Vilma's legs, pecking, pecking, pecking. Even Mr. Pelletier, who didn't really remember who he was, flew around Vilma's head, attacking her.

Janice balled herself up in a fetal position, but then she went board-straight and stiff. Instead of her neon-blue sneakers, she had bright orange bird feet the size of catchers' mitts, four bony toes pointing in different directions. Every time the B-team pulled at her she shrieked because they were hurting her without meaning to. So they stopped and just stood there, shaking, hands over their mouths.

As I watched, my sister's legs went orange and shrank down skinny as a stair rail. "Janice!" I screamed. "No!" I threw myself at Vilma but she pushed me away so hard I fell down.

Mim crouched beside me. "What . . . Janice . . . what."

"Let go of her!" Hillyard attached himself to Vilma's arm, but she shoved him away too.

Janice was on her back, her arms spread out flat except they were these huge wings, black on the bottom, white on top. Vilma called out, "A stork she shall be, like we have across the sea." Janice arched her back and opened her mouth to scream, but no sound came out. She was feathers from the neck down.

Mim let out a yell and launched herself, crashing into Vilma with the full force of an angry carpenter, and the B-team was on Vilma again, too, hauling her away from Janice, chickens pecking, pecking.

Mim got Janice under the wings, pulled her over to the henhouse.

Vilma started a different chant, loud, louder, arms up, her face to the sky.

"Hillyard," I yelled, "I think she's calling Margily."

Janice was sobbing now, lying there all stork except her head. I dropped to my knees. "I'm sorry," I wailed. "I'm so sorry."

She tried to talk but nothing came out. I wiped the tears off her cheek but they kept coming. The B-team was with us, clutching at each other, eyes wide and scared.

Whump, whump, whump.

Margily.

Margily would help.

The birds shrieked and disappeared under the henhouse. Mim made a gargling noise and sat down next to Janice because there was this amazing dragon soaring towards us all gorgeous and ginormous.

"Ohhhhhh." I think that was Taylor.

"Don't worry," I said to Mim. "She's friendly."

"Don't be so sure, little girl," Vilma snarled.

Yes. We are friends.

Mim clapped her hands to her ears. "What was that?" Her eyes were wild. "It's in my head!"

"The dragon is telepathic," Hillyard said.

Like any part of *that* sentence made sense.

Margily cupped her wings, reaching down with her back feet. The spicy, swampy smell blew over us as her feet landed at the far end of Vilma's yard, her tail making an ugly mess of the neighbor's tulip bed.

"Donna-a-a-a," Mim moaned. "I didn't believe you about the dragon."

I hardly ever saw Margily in daytime. I was knocked out all over again by her beauty, so shiny green and red, her scales like jewels. "Ma-a-a-an," I breathed.

"Beautiful." Taylor again.

Your admiration is appreciated.

"This child stole my gold!" Vilma hollered.

I am shocked.

"How did she hide it from me all this time? Why did I sense it only this hour?"

Margily was silent.

"For that matter, how did she know where to find my book?"

Silence.

Vilma slapped Margily on the nose. "*You* helped her. Why would you do this?"

Margily stared at her, cobalt blue. Then she put her head up and blasted steam straight at the sky. Vilma took a step backwards.

Why? You ask WHY? Because it is wrong, old woman, to change a living creature into something else. It is an affront to magic. You're not even good at it. Look at those poor raccoons you tried to turn into household items.

Oh. The table with raccoon feet. The mug with ears. The *slippers*, for Pete's sake.

The girl has been trying to save her friend who is now a bird and, yes, I helped her.

"Lizard," Vilma said. "I am your master, though I have been a lenient one. I order you now, bring me that girl, that I may take my vengeance on her. The boy too."

No.

"I hereby exert my control." Vilma raised her book higher, said a word that made Margily shudder from her head to the tip of her tail.

No, she whispered.

Vilma spoke the word again. Margily gasped and ducked her head.

"Do it," Vilma said. "*Now.*"

Trembling, Margily turned her huge head to look at me, eyes gleaming. *This will make me sad.*

But Vilma didn't reckon on pixies. A whirling tornado

of tiny lights surged up around her like a swarm of mosquitoes. She dropped her book and swatted at them like a madwoman.

And she didn't reckon on Nancy Jane Landon, who was fed up in ways even a dragon couldn't understand. "Not Donna too!" Mim yelled, and she had my hand and she pulled me down the hillside steps, my feet barely touching the ground. "I'll be back, Janice!" she hollered over her shoulder.

"Get that child!" Vilma screamed.

We were in our dooryard. We were almost to the house.

Margily roared and something crashed onto the ground right behind us. Because we were nuts, we turned to look. Margily's head and forelegs were in our yard, her huge body covering the steps. Her jaws could reach us, easy.

Mim let go my hand and turned to face the dragon. "Donna, get inside!" she shouted.

But I couldn't because there was Hillyard, climbing down Margily like she was the steps. I don't know what he thought he could do to help, but I wasn't going to leave him out there, was I?

"Hurry up, Hillyard!" I screamed, but it was too late. Margily's big head lunged for me, teeth bared, knocking Mim out of the way. The spicy smell flooded over me, but those teeth, oh jeez'm, two rows of them, long and sharp. I closed my eyes.

Get on. You and the boy. Now!

I opened my eyes. Cobalt blue. "What about Janice?"

We'll think of something. Do as I say! Before Madame collects herself!

She crouched, one leg out for me to climb on. Not wasting a second, I scrambled up and found a seat between two spikes at the bottom of her neck. Hillyard was already two spaces behind me.

"Donna!" my mother shrieked. "Get off of there!"

I waved like a little kid on a merry-go-round so she'd see I was okay. Margily lumbered to the front dooryard, unfurled her wings—*fwap!*—and flew over the road, barely clearing the rosebushes. She glided out over the water.

Vilma shrieked, and Margily's flight pattern went all wrong. She flapped, flapped, flapped, trying to rise up from the river, then jolted downwards, barely staying out of the water. It was hard to hold on.

"What's wrong with you?" I yelled.

Madame Vilma. She is summoning me. It is hard to resist. Margily gave a gasp, as if she were in pain. *It's hard even to think. I shall have to land you somewhere and . . . No!*

She flipped upside down.

Off I went, head first.

CHAPTER TWENTY

The Drowning

And I was in the water, under the water, thrashing for air. Then my head was up and I was breathing, breathing—but I couldn't see Hillyard and the current had me, rushing me down to bridges and barges and the open sea. I tried to do the breaststroke and aim for shore but it wasn't working.

Look out, Petunia!

Margily was over my head, but she was going down, down. She hit the water about twenty feet away. The wave swamped me and pushed me under. Everything was bubbles and murk and I didn't know what was up and what was down.

Stop panicking, Petunia. A voice in my head, but it wasn't Margily. It was different, even more familiar, part of me. *Let the river take care of you,* the voice said. *Drift.*

Annabelle. Was she in my head all along?

I did what I was told: I stopped thrashing and let myself drift, and I saw there was light overhead so I kicked for it and then my face was out, under a new sky. I coughed and coughed, but water kept going up my nose so probably I was going to drown anyways.

I'm coming. Something was rising up under me, something huge, terrifying. But, oh, it was Margily, and Hillyard was next to me, the two of us on our stomachs across her back, coughing and gasping.

We were in the air again, flying smooth enough so me and Hillyard could wiggle around and get seated between spikes. We couldn't hear Vilma shrieking anymore. "Maybe she . . . gave up?" Hillyard choked out.

Don't think it for a minute. Margily flapped up until she was high above the river, heading south. *We need to get away.*

"North," I croaked, shoving my wet hair out of my eyes. "Not as many people."

North it is. She wheeled around.

But something was wrong again. Margily gasped, and her wing beats faltered.

There was a black speck in the air over my house, coming for us fast. "What's that?" I whispered, but of course I knew.

Madame Vilma can fly when she has her book in her hand.

"Can you outrun her?"

Not like this. Margily was skipping every other wing beat. The river was getting closer again.

"She's catching up," Hillyard said.

We could see Vilma clearly now, her book in hand. She was almost on us, her soft blue shirt rippling under her wool vest.

Hang on! Margily launched into a series of sickening dives and twists. I clung to the spike in front of me and shut my eyes.

Which is why I never knew when Vilma caught us.

One second I was clinging to Margily, trying not to whimper. Next second something had me by the arm and I opened my eyes and it was Vilma, sitting behind me, her hand digging into me, burning, burning, and she was chanting. My head went fuzzy and my fingers went all prickly and when I looked down they weren't fingers. They were feathers.

We were over the rapids. About ten feet over them, to be exact.

"Shall I drop you into this turbulence?" Vilma said in my ear. I writhed in her grasp, but I was burning, burning like I hugged a woodstove—hurt too much even to yell, hurt too much to think, and my left arm was a wing.

To mothproof woolen clothes, wrap them in newspaper,

Margily whispered. *Too much detergent in the washer? A sprinkle of salt will settle the suds.*

"Margily," I gasped. "What the heck . . . ?" I had one orange foot now.

Can't think . . . Trying to find something . . . in Annabelle's book. Her next wing-flap actually touched the rapids, but she surged up again, breathing hard.

Hillyard yelled like he was sledding on a steep hill. "AAAAHHHHHH!!!"

"Get this off!" Vilma hollered. She jerked and thrashed behind me.

Because she had a purple, gold, and royal blue fringed scarf wrapped twice around her eyes and nose.

But she still had her hand on me, burning, burning.

River runs free, like a glittering seam of stars. The poem Annabelle always shouted on Table Rock, the one she copied into the back of the Guide. The rapids were so close. We were almost in them.

"Annabelle," I whispered. She loved this river, but that didn't save her. I was so *mad* about so many things: Annabelle going kayaking that day, Cousin Betty butting in all the time, Rachel not being my friend. Mim working so hard and never talking about her sister. I was mad at those rapids down there, because they started it.

And that old woman behind me, with her horrible book.

I never liked stories about magic stored in some object another person could destroy. Annabelle's Guide said that about pixies. *Better to rely on yourself.*

"Gahhhhh!" I let out a yell and slammed my free elbow backwards, where I thought that book might be, with all its flimsy paper.

Found it.

Vilma shrieked so loud it made my ears ring. Her book arced away from us into the air. She lunged after it but she couldn't see where it was because of Hillyard's scarf over her eyes. She lunged too far. She fell over. And of course she couldn't fly without her book.

Down, down she went, arms and legs flailing.

A geyser of water flew up where the book hit. Thunder clapped. Lightning flashed. Vilma hit the water a second later. Hillyard whooped. "Yay, river!"

Her book! Margily cried. *It's dissolved!*

Sure enough I had my arm back, feather-free. Which was good, because Margily spun into a nosedive, and jeez'm, we needed to hang on tight. Margily snagged Vilma's vest in her teeth and headed south for home.

The vest came off about twenty feet from Table Rock. With a cry of rage, Vilma splashed back into the water, went under, came up gasping. The scarf came off too.

She can make it to shore from there, Margily said, cupping her wings to land in our dooryard. She knelt so me and Hillyard could slide down. *Sorry about that beautiful scarf.*

My feet barely hit the ground when somebody threw herself at me so hard we both slammed into Margily's side. Somebody with blaze-orange hair and not a feather on her. Hugging me so hard I could barely breathe.

"I'm not a bird!" Janice yelled. "What did you do?"

"She knocked Vilma's book right out of her hand!" Hillyard was dancing around us. "It fell in the river. So did Vilma!"

"Because you wrapped your scarf around her eyes!" I was dancing too, but I'm not so good at it and Janice gave this hoot of laughter. "I'm sorry you got turned into a bird," I said.

"I didn't though, did I?" She tried to hug me again but I was dancing.

"Donna!" Mim was on us, hauling me away from Margily and Hillyard, ending the dance. "I can't believe you got on that dragon. How could you be so stupid?"

"Mim." I dug in my heels. "Margily's my friend. She was flying us *away* from Vilma." I wriggled out of her grasp and stepped back, colliding with Margily's snout.

"Vilma caught up, though," Hillyard said. "She almost turned Donna into a stork. She had feathers and everything."

Mim swayed. Janice held her up. "I know it doesn't make a lot of sense, Mim. But you get used to it."

On the riverbank, a dripping Vilma hauled herself out of the water. "Welp, you certainly fixed *her*," Janice said.

Mim jerked away from Janice. "I'm going to give that woman a piece of my mind."

"Donna already took care of that, Mim." Janice grabbed her arm. Vilma limped over the rocks, collapsed to her knees, and crashed down on her stomach. She must've been pretty wiped out.

I was starting to notice something. Crowd noises, at Vilma's. "What's going on up there?" I asked Janice.

"Hoo-boy. Wait'll you see."

Me and Hillyard and Janice and Mim made for the hillside steps. Rachel and the B-team were there and when Rachel saw me she ran down and threw her arms around me.

"Thank you," she whispered. "Whatever you did." She was messy and dirty and she smelled like a hen-house. Some of her hair was still feathers, but it looked pretty. I eased her away from me. "Are you okay?"

She nodded and took a deep breath. "Donna. I didn't notice how sad you still were." I shrugged like it was nothing, but she shook her head. "No. I should've asked. Guess I listen better when I'm a chicken."

That was nice, but . . . I took my own deep breath,

turned so Hillyard could hear me too. "My brain told Vilma to turn you into a hen. I didn't really mean to." I looked at Rachel. "Also, I guess I *talk* better when you're a chicken."

Rachel hugged me again and whispered, "You're not a loser."

I gave her a squeeze and turned to Hillyard. "I said no to Vilma out loud but yes in my head. Margily told Vilma I wanted to do it."

Oh, of course. Blame it on me.

"I lied to you," I told Hillyard, making sure he understood what a bad thing I did.

He stood there a minute, frowning. But then he said, "I see how that could happen."

"You're an amazing friend, Hillyard."

Rachel fished around in her pocket, pulled out an elastic, wiped some feather crud off it. "Turn around." She gave me a super-fast sort of a braid.

Then she hugged Hillyard.

Hippie Hillyard, who nobody talked to.

You never saw anybody so red in the ears as he was. The sides of his mouth kept curling up.

I got hugged by all three B-teamers at the top of the steps, even Taylor. She said, "Can I hang out with Margily?"

"Don't ask me."

You are welcome to visit with me.

"Awesome." Taylor ran down the steps.

She smiled at Hillyard on the way down. Mei Xing did too. So did Sarah, and for a second it looked like she was going to hug him but she changed her mind. Just as well, because I think he might have fainted.

The whole neighborhood was milling around in Vilma's dooryard. Hillyard's parents came rushing over and did a group hug, sort of a Hillyard sandwich. His mom had her hand in a cast. My mom went over to talk to her and Mr. Martin.

Mr. Pelletier, Aunt Dana, Mr. Altin, and two ladies I didn't know were sitting by the henhouse, totally messy like Rachel. Aunt Dana didn't look so bad, but Mr. Altin, Mr. Pelletier, and the ladies had feathers poking out all over the place. "Nothing a good pair of tweezers won't fix," Janice whispered.

The police chief was on Vilma's back steps, waving his arms for quiet. The local game warden, Annabelle's friend Arthur Libby, hunkered down at the foot of the steps, leafing through his big book.

"Folks, folks. Folks!" Chief Wilson bellowed. "Simmer down. Please. Simmer down." He blew his whistle. "Now, we all saw something . . . something strange going on with Rachel and Mr. Pelletier and the ladies. And that . . . that thing flying around. And I understand from Mrs. Wells"—he nodded at the lady from across the street, who kept scowling at the B-team—"that the thing flew away with Donna Landon."

"And blew steam out its mouth," Mrs. Wells shouted. "And it took that Martin boy too . . . oh." She caught sight of me and Hillyard. "Here they are back again."

"I don't want to scare nobody," another neighbor said. "But the thing's right down there in the Landons' dooryard and Taylor's on top of it."

Warden Libby sped up his page-flipping.

"Got anything, Libby?" the chief asked. "Tranquilizer or something?"

The warden shook his head. "I know how much'll knock out a moose. How many moose you figure that thing adds up to?"

A spicy, swampy smell wafted over us, and there was Margily, front feet on either side of the hillside steps, head poking up over the crest of the hill, Taylor on her back, beaming. The crowd opened their mouths to scream.

Hello, good people.

Everybody clapped their hands over their ears.

Please do not be alarmed. I am friendly, for the most part. Donna and Hillyard will assure you that I mean no harm to anyone. The child Taylor is on my back by her own choice.

"It's true! She's friendly!" I shouted. "See, Hillyard and I are fine. We rode on her and everything, and we're . . . we're . . ."

"Alive," Hillyard said.

"Why'd that thing take you away, though?" Mrs. Wells yelled. "Answer me that."

I apologize for any distress I may have caused. I was trying to save Donna and Hillyard from being turned into storks like Donna's sister, you see.

Well, that shut everybody up.

Here. I'll show you the real culprit. Margily's head disappeared, popped up again with Vilma dangling from her teeth by the belt of her leather trousers. Margily dropped her on all fours next to me and Hillyard. *This is Madame Vilma. She is a thunder mage, and she—*

Whump, whump, whump. Whump, whump, whump, whump, whump, whump, whump . . .

Something loomed over us. We all looked up at a sound like a thousand eagles flying over our heads.

Ohhhhhh, man.

CHAPTER TWENTY-ONE
Madame Sarika

A shiny purple dragon hovered overhead, wings cupped for landing.

Hah. I thought this might happen. If she was paying attention, she knew where to find Madame Vilma the minute you said her name with her book in your hands. That's why Madame was so angry.

"She who?" I whispered.

Petunia, dear. That dragon has riders.

Margily lifted her gorgeous green head and locked eyes with the purple dragon. It flapped down close enough to touch noses with her, then slid away on the air to land down in our yard, on the trunk of the fallen maple tree. It broke in half with a gunshot snap.

Sure enough, she had somebody on her back. Two somebodies: a tall lady in leather, with a man behind her clutching a spine-spike for dear life. The man had feathers for hair and large orange bird feet.

Oh dear, Margily murmured. *Madame Sarika's husband still has some avian qualities, doesn't he?*

"Did Vilma change him—?"

Into a stork. Just before she absconded with the gold. He was a stork for so long, it seems he didn't change back completely. They'll have to work on getting rid of those feet.

Vilma yelped and ran for her kitchen door. When she opened it, five raccoons tumbled down the back steps and zipped into the crowd. They zoomed around the house and headed for the woods behind Mrs. Wells's house across the street.

The lock clicked shut on Vilma's kitchen door.

Madame Sarika jumped off her dragon and made for the hill. Margily still blocked the hillside steps, so Madame Sarika floated up to where we stood in Vilma's yard, holding a leather book like Vilma's.

The man with the stork feet stayed down in our yard with the purple dragon.

Taylor, sitting on Margily's back but gazing at the purple dragon, looked happier than I'd ever seen her. The other B-teamers and our neighbors stood around with their mouths open, brain-frozen.

Madame Sarika looked younger than Vilma. She had the brightest light-blue eyes you ever saw and a cute little pointy nose like a Disney fairy. But the look in her eye was anything but Disney—baleful, I'd have to say.

Margily inclined her head to her. *Madame Sarika, allow me to present my friends Donna Landon and Hillyard Martin. Donna lives in the house on whose grounds you have landed. She has drowned Madame Vilma's book.*

Madame Sarika gave a start, and thrust her head forward so our noses almost touched. She rapped out something I couldn't understand.

"Uh-oh," Hillyard whispered.

Margily turned her head slightly, so I could see her cobalt eyes. *Regrettably, Madame Sarika does not have her sister's aptitude for human language. She wants to know if you make a practice of destroying thunder mages. Shall I tell her no?*

Madame Sarika was giving me the stink eye something fierce. But I was done getting the stink eye from thunder mages. "Depends," I said.

I guess Margily mind-spoke something more soothing, because Madame lost interest in me. She marched off to Vilma's back steps, waggled her fingers to undo the lock, and pushed through the door.

The crowd was stunned quiet. So we heard every word when the shouting started inside, even though we didn't understand any of it. Man, they were ticked off. Somebody was sobbing—Vilma? Really?

As you may have guessed, Madame Sarika is Madame Vilma's younger sister, Margily explained, I guess just to me and maybe Hillyard, because none of the grown-ups clapped their hands on their ears. *I imagine she's been looking for her sister for some time now. She's every bit as possessed by that gold as Madame Vilma is.*

Since Margily and the new dragon hadn't eaten anybody yet, our neighbors were calming down. Arthur Libby, the game warden, started across towards me and Hillyard, saw how close we were to Margily's snout, and beckoned us to him. "Donna, can you give me an idea what's going on, dear?"

I didn't know just where to start. "Um. Well. Vilma Bliksem is a thunder mage and Margily is her dragon." Figured I'd keep it simple.

"Margily *was* her dragon," Hillyard butted in. "I think she's free now that there's no book."

"Right. Anyways, Vilma came here because she turned some guy into a stork and stole gold, which is a bad thing for a thunder mage—"

"Or anybody," Hillyard muttered.

"Right. And it looks like her sister came to get her. Vilma doesn't have any power anymore because her magic book got disintegrated in the river—"

"Because Donna whapped it out of her hand," Hillyard said.

"Right. Anyways, I'm pretty sure the mages and the dragons will all go back home now, so we should leave them alone and not ask for trouble."

"Let 'em get on with it, that's what you're saying?"

I waved my hand at Margily and the purple dragon. "Look how gorgeous they are." Warden Libby gave a weak nod. "They aren't going to hurt anybody. They'll leave soon as Vilma's sister gets done yelling at her."

"Plus," Hillyard added, "you don't want to make them mad. The dragons and the mages, they can make thunderstorms. And turn people into birds. And give bad luck."

That made the warden's eyes pop out a tetch. "I thought you said they wouldn't hurt anyone."

"Well, it's true you don't want to tick them off," I said. "Otherwise they're fine."

"We should let them go home," Hillyard said.

Warden Libby let out a long breath. "This better be all right, Donna. My neck's on the line here." He started back towards Chief Wilson.

"It'll be fine—" I started to say, but Vilma's back door burst open. Madame Sarika stepped out and waved me to her. Hillyard came with me.

She wishes to address the crowd, Margily said. *I will translate her words and send them to you, so you can speak for her in English. My mind-speaking seems to upset the adults.*

Everybody was looking at me. The whole neighborhood. Rachel and the B-team. Everybody. "Uh," I said to them all. "Madame Sarika wants to talk to you and I'm going to, um . . ."

Translate.

"I'm going to translate," I said.

"Can't hear you!" Mrs. Wells yelled.

I swallowed a fear lump, took a deep breath, and said it again, super loud.

Dead silence and a dooryard full of eyeballs.

Madame Sarika spoke, and a minute later Margily was in my mind. I translated. "So, she says she's sorry for the trouble Vil—uh, Ms. Bliksem . . . uh, sorry for the trouble she caused and for how scary it is to see your first dragon, even when the dragon is as spectacular as Margily." I doubted Madame Sarika ever said that last bit about being spectacular but what the heck.

"The dragons and Ms. Bliksem will be going home now, across the sea. So, you know, we don't have to worry about them anymore."

"Awwww." Taylor looked like somebody outlawed the jump shot.

Madame Sarika spoke some more. I translated some more: "So, Madame Sarika says we probably shouldn't tell anybody about these dragons because everybody will think we've lost our minds."

"Sad but true," Mim said, smiling at me.

"Plus, if we agree to keep our mouths shut, she and Ms. Bliksem will offer double good luck to everybody in town for one year, starting today."

"Double good luck?" Mrs. Wells said. "What does that mean?"

"Never seen the good luck, but I sure can vouch for the bad version." I waved my arm at our dead maple tree and even deader red truck.

Nobody looked too convinced. "Margily," I whispered, "can Madame Sarika show them some good luck?"

It took a minute for Margily to translate, but then the tall woman smiled. *I have made a suggestion,* Margily said, *based on time spent in your head.*

"Madame Sarika," I announced, "is going to show you some luck."

We waited. Everybody watched everybody else for signs of luck, although I don't know what they were expecting except maybe golden earmuffs.

Hillyard slid over to the foot of the steps. "What's happening?" he whispered.

"I don't kn—"

A shriek split the air. Annie, the high school girl who lived down the street, ran her hands over her face and squealed. "My zits are gone! They're all gone!" She ran for her house, weeping—for joy, I guess, because I doubt anybody misses their zits.

"Donna," Mrs. Wells called. "Ask her if she can do anything about unsightly hand moles."

Tell her yes.

"Yes," I said. Mrs. Wells held her hands up in front of her face, and a minute later she yelled and slumped to the ground in a dead faint. The guy standing next to her peered down at her hands. "Yep," he said. "Nary a mole."

Wallace Millikin, who lived next to Mr. Pelletier, was babbling away on his cell phone. He stuck it in his pocket and called to his wife across the yard. "Judy! I got that job." Mrs. Millikin burst into tears, exactly like Annie.

Madame Sarika spoke. *She says that's just the beginning,* Margily relayed.

"And that's just the beginning!" I yelled.

"Think she's got herself a deal," Warden Libby said.

Wallace Millikin shoved through the crowd towards the pricker-bush path. "Don't know about you folks, but I'm buying a lottery ticket."

Well, didn't that clear the crowd out.

CHAPTER TWENTY-TWO

Goodbye

Y ou'd think a woman would be happy her daughters weren't turned into storks. Mim did not look
happy.

"Sit down," she said when we got to the kitchen.
"Both of you."

"Mim," I said. "I'm really tired. Plus, isn't it way past
lunchtime?"

"I can be emancipated," Janice said. "I'm sixteen."

"Sit. Down."

So we sat.

Mim sat too. She folded her hands on the table. "Talk.
From the beginning. Do not leave out anything."

So we told her. All of it, even me turning Rachel into
a chicken and stealing a sack of gold.

Mim slumped back in her chair. "I was worried about

beer and cigarettes—I never considered felony theft." She looked at me. "You stole from *an old lady*."

"I was taking action. You said—"

The look on Mim's face froze the words on my tongue. "I did not tell you 'taking action' meant stealing from the neighbors."

"Rachel was a *chicken*."

Mim couldn't help it—she grinned. I hadn't seen that face in *so* long. "Strong excuse, I admit."

We didn't tell her how hard I tried to keep the gold for myself. Some things are more than a mother needs to know.

As it was, she had to sit for a while looking at nothing. Then she scrubbed her face with her hands like she was waking up. "Okay. You were trying to help. I know that." She stood up. "But this is still the real world, and it turns out somebody wants to buy this house. We have to leave when school's over."

Janice and me, we sat there stunned—after all we went through, nothing changed?

Mim headed for the living room. "I'm going to pack some more. You two grab something to eat and take a quick nap, then come help me." She walked out.

Seriously. Weren't *we* going to get any good luck?

* * *

Lying on my bed, listening to the rapids, Ursa Major above me, I wondered if any human being was ever this tired in the history of the world.

Sad, too. We were moving and Margily was leaving and I was never going to hear her voice in my head again. We don't realize how alone we are, all this skull between us and everybody else.

Many people actually like being alone in their heads. You did, before I arrived.

"Can you talk to me from home?"

No, no. That would mean I could hear every thought in the world. I'd go, as you say, nuts. You might consider sharing your thoughts with your fellow humans. They're nowhere near as intelligent or insightful as a dragon, but it'll be better than nothing.

I buried my face in my pillow.

Come to the river at sunset. You and Hillyard. Madame Sarika won't want to leave until full dark. We'll fly one more time.

I dozed off, dreamed about flying over the Maine woods.

The phone woke me up. Mim got it in the living room, the murmur of her voice rising now and then to something I could hear: "You're kidding," and "Well, thanks." That got me up.

In the living room, Mim was looking out over the

river, phone to her ear. Janice was on the stairs in her sleep shirt.

Mim listened and listened. She took a deep breath, crossed her fingers behind her back, and said, "I'm going to need more than that. I've been having trouble making ends meet over here. I'm worth more. And I'll be a better employee if I'm not working three jobs."

I crossed my fingers. So did Janice. "Luck," I whispered.

Luck, Margily whispered back. *And courage.*

"That's fine," Mim said. "We'll talk about it tomorrow. See you then."

She hung up the phone, turned around.

"You got your job back," Janice said. "And maybe more money."

Mim sat down on the couch. "They offered it, but it might make sense to get out of here and start over someplace else." She shivered. "That river out there. It's not friendly."

Janice went to sit next to her on the couch. "Annabelle loved the river."

"And it drowned her," Mim whispered.

"It wasn't the river's fault," I said. "Anyways, *I* love this river. And"—I swallowed hard—"I'm not leaving it without a fight."

"Me neither," Janice said. "You're not in this alone, you know, Mim."

Pretty close to what Annabelle wrote to Mim, before I was even born.

"Hang on." I ran to my room and found the pages with Annabelle's writing: the letter about grieving and the Guide stuff about pixies. Back in the living room, I flung them on the coffee table in front of Mim. "We're not babies. You didn't have to hide this stuff."

Mim looked at those papers like they came from Mars. "Where did you find these?"

"That's Annabelle's writing," Janice said, lunging for the letter.

"You had me pack up your desk, remember?" I said to Mim. "I read it all. Annabelle *told* you to let other people help you."

"*Don't retreat into yourself the way you always do,*" Janice read from the page in her hand.

"And for your information, pixies helped save us—today and all week," I said. "We need to know things. We can *handle* knowing things."

Mim gave a little snort. "Well, you don't need Cousin Betty to toughen you up, that's for sure." Her eyes got watery. "I can't tell you how proud that makes me."

Janice finished reading. "Why'd you hide this stuff?"

Mim shook her head—at herself, I think. "I forgot about that letter. And"—she straightened her backbone—"I certainly didn't want you running around believing in pixies." We stared at her and she looked embarrassed. "Seems silly now, doesn't it?"

She picked up Annabelle's letter about grief, put it on her knee, smoothed out the wrinkles. "We'll put this in the Guide."

"The pixie stuff too," I said.

She nodded, reached out to grab Janice's hand.

Janice didn't pull away. "Mim, when's the last time you went down to the river?"

"Not since . . ." She didn't have to finish that sentence. We knew what she meant.

"Pixies live in those houses we built," I said. "Annabelle knew that."

Mim stood up, looked out the window at Table Rock. "I think I knew it too."

"I'm going down at sunset to say goodbye to Margily," I said softly. "Come with me?"

She nodded.

"Great," Janice said. "Another lizard encounter."

Nobody said you had to come.

"I'll be there, lizard."

Mim joined us, but she stayed up by the rosebushes. When Margily burst from the water, me and Hillyard were out on Table Rock, Janice at the edge of the riverbank with her arms folded, looking like she smelled something. Which we all did, but I liked it.

Margily sidled up to the rock. *Climb on, one last time. The unpleasant older sister too.*

"No way," Janice said. "I did it once and that was enough."

That was business. This is pleasure. You should not let such chances pass you by, no matter how small-minded you may be.

"Come on," I said. "You know it's safe."

"I didn't puke," Hillyard said, "and I got sick on a kiddie Ferris wheel."

Janice looked at Mim. "I will if you will."

"Oh, no, no, no," Mim said. She looked like *she* might puke. Don't forget, a day ago she was a nonfiction person. *Please, Nan. I think you'll enjoy it.*

I climbed up Margily's forearm and nestled between the spikes at the base of her neck. "Look. It's easy."

"And," Hillyard said, "I didn't—"

"If you say 'puke' again I'm throwing you in the river." Janice took Mim by the hand.

"I can't believe I'm doing this," Mim said.

When they got out on the rock, Hillyard offered his hand like a gentleman to help Janice climb up. She looked at him like he was a bug and climbed to the spike behind me. Mim did take his hand, but I think she was being polite—she could totally get up there on her own. She sat behind Janice, Hillyard behind her.

Margily eased away from the rock and unfolded her giant bat wings. Mim gave a little moan.

I do not let people fall.

"What about the smell?" Janice muttered.

There are, of course, exceptions to every rule.

The wings flapped, flapped, flapped, Margily's back muscles pumping under us. We rose from the water, picked up speed.

Then. Oh, then.

Joy, Margily said.

Joy, my thoughts answered.

"Yahoooooo!" Hillyard yelled.

The river sank beneath us. I spread my arms wide, letting the wind rush at every part of me as Margily headed north to the great woods.

"Children," Mim said. "Please hang on."

"It's fine," I called back to her.

No, she's right. Hang on. I'm going to swoop.

She tilted right and, oh, jeez'm, what a swoop. My stomach dropped out from under me and Janice screamed as we swept across the river. We straightened out, tilted the other way to cross back, and up the river we went, swooping from side to side.

Janice went quiet. I twisted to look at her and her

face was calm, watching the woods go by. "Cool, right?" I called.

She shrugged. But I knew darn well it was very, very cool.

"It's very cool," Mim said.

Darkness came down. Stars popped into view. A half-moon came up, shimmering on the ocean far to our east. I got thinking about how I'd never do this again and it was so sad I almost cried.

Never say never. I am no longer bonded to Madame Vilma—your doing, dear, because you destroyed her book. Perhaps I will come back for a visit. And of course you will travel the world. Perhaps our paths will cross.

I didn't think of that. Maybe I *would* travel the world.

Stranger things have happened.

We swept back up the river by moonlight. Mim moaned again as we came in for a landing. Splashdown made Janice swear because she got her sneakers wet. There's no pleasing some people.

As we slid off Margily, Mim looked the huge dragon in the eye. "I never thanked you for taking care of my children."

It was my pleasure, Nan.

We stood there quiet, gazing at the dim path of

moonlight on the river. You could see the water rippling through it, tipped with light.

"A glittering seam of stars," Mim murmured. Her eyes were shiny, like they had tears in them.

"That's what Annabelle said," I whispered.

Mim nodded. And that's when I knew we had a chance.

Janice got Annabelle's measuring cup and filled all the little rock bowls by the pixie houses.

I said, "Somebody's been doing that, I think."

"No kidding."

What. "That was *you?*"

She filled the last one, put the measuring cup back in its place. "Well, I wasn't going to let them dry up, was I?" She wiped her hands on her pants. "I'm going home and changing my shoes. Come on, Nancy Jane. Let Donna say goodbye to the dragon."

Goodbye, Petunia's older sister.

Janice turned and bowed—I wasn't sure whether she was mocking or not. "Thank you for not dropping me into the river." It was too dark to tell, but I think she smirked. "Lizard."

"Janice!" Mim said.

Janice hooked her arm in Mim's and marched for the rosebushes, the road, and home.

Abominable girl. But Margily didn't sound angry.

Hillyard and I stood there on the rock. I didn't know what to do. Part of me wanted to . . . I dunno, hug Margily, although my arms would never reach around her neck.

You may stroke my snout if you wish.

I guess Hillyard heard that too, because he put out his hand for the one smooth place on Margily's head, the top of her nose between her nostrils. She pushed her head forward so he could reach.

"Wow," he said, stroking. "It's like satin or something."

Margily let him give a few more strokes, then said softly, *It has been a pleasure knowing you, Hillyard. Now, if you wouldn't mind, perhaps you should go home and be with your parents. They've been worried about you.*

Hillyard stepped back and looked at me. "Dad got in touch with the Wittinghams, and he talked them into letting us finish the henhouse. He told them it would add value to the property. We can talk about it at school, I guess."

"Okay."

"He says, soon as you're old enough for a work permit, he could use an assistant. And you can hang out with us this summer, help with chores if you want." He looked at his feet. "So, you know, you don't have to go to Cousin Betty's."

I couldn't believe I ever wanted Hillyard's dad to butt out. "That's amazing, Hillyard. Thanks." I watched him go, his sequined sneakers winking in the moonlight.

Will you keep me company until we leave, Petunia?

I sat down on the rock. The moon rose higher. Margily lowered the tip of her chin onto my lap and closed her eyes, and we were silent, even in our heads, though Margily's mind-voice was humming something, a lullaby.

For the first time since Annabelle died, my eyes filled with tears. Something important was about to be ripped out of me—maybe Margily's voice in my head, maybe Annabelle's, maybe both of them, intertwined like a length of rope.

Annabelle is here. She's in her book.

"Books can be destroyed," I whispered.

Well, I found Annabelle's book in your head. And that's where I found her. She's in this river, too.

"Margily, was it . . . was it you who told me to let the river take care of me? When I went under?"

It wasn't.

"It seemed like it was Annabelle."

Margily didn't say anything for a minute. Then: *Love is a mystery. I suppose your Annabelle is part of this river because she loved it so much. She's part of you for the same reason. Always will be.*

But her hugs—those were gone for good.

There will be other hugs. I promise, Petunia.

I was leaning back on my arms, my eyes closed, almost dozing, when there was a *sploosh*.

I scrambled to my feet as a dark, huge, glistening body made its way to Table Rock.

That spicy, swampy dragon smell. I was going to miss it.

The purple dragon eased up to Margily. They rubbed their spiky cheeks together, making a sound like sandpaper. *Sofia*, Margily said, *this is my friend Donna. Donna, this is Sofia, my sister.*

A ruby-red eye appeared over the top of Margily's head. I gave a little wave. "Hello. Nice to meet you."

Sofia made a noise that sounded an awful lot like a growl. I took a step backwards.

Stop it, Sofia. Margily prodded the purple dragon with her snout. *I apologize for my sister, Donna. She thinks she's being funny.* Her mind-voice dropped to a whisper. *This is another thing we have in common—abominable sisters.*

Gravel crunched behind me. *Ah. Here come their high haunchinesses.*

Vilma and Madame Sarika struggled through the rosebushes, carrying a heavy chest with handles. The gold, I guessed. Sarika's poor husband flapped along behind them on his orange stork feet.

Vilma stopped next to me. She wouldn't look at me. "I apologize." She shot an evil look at Madame Sarika. "There, I said it. Satisfied?"

Sisters. Jeez'm.

Still not looking at me, Vilma said, "I must go home to help cure the stork-man, perhaps reclaim some of my magic. But I will be back."

"Y-you will?"

She won't.

Vilma climbed up to sit at Margily's neck, and now she looked at me. "I do not need gold, and I do not need a dragon."

She does.

Vilma shot me her pencil-jab smile. "I will work at L.L.Bean."

Sofia sidled up to the end of the rock. Madame Sarika walked down there, her husband flapping behind.

Vilma leaned down from her seat at Margily's neck. "Pixies," she said in a low voice.

What was I supposed to say to that? "Yeah? So?"

She leaned closer. "The biggest little house."

"What the heck does that—"

Madame Sarika rapped out some sort of command. Margily moved away from the rock.

"Ms. Bliksem," I called. "What did you mean?"

But Margily was heading out to the middle of the river. I ran to the end of the rock to watch her glide away from me, pacing along the river bottom until she was deep enough to swim.

Her huge wings unfurled, spraying droplets, then flapped. She rose from the water, moving faster, faster, faster. Up she went, wings beating the air with a grace that made my throat hurt.

Joy.

Whump, whump, whump. Her sister joined Margily in the air, scales glinting, the two of them swooping, weaving, looking for the right air current. They found it. They straightened out, flapping, gliding, flapping. They headed east, towards the sunrise.

Goodbye, Petunia. You are loved.

Janice came to get me from Table Rock. It must've been midnight. I was lying on my side shivering and listening to the rapids. They didn't have much to say: just *yes-s-s-s.*

"Mim says you better sleep some." But Janice sat down next to me. "And we're eating breakfast together. New rules." She hesitated. "You're gonna miss that dragon, I guess."

I sat up, hugging my knees. Man, I was cold. "When she started talking to me, it was like Annabelle's voice was coming from the rapids."

Janice pulled something out of her pocket, held it out in the moonlight. Annabelle's purple socks with gold stars. "I sleep with them under my pillow. They smell like lavender." She held the socks to her nose.

"Feeling anxious?" I whispered. "Rub lavender oil on your temples."

Janice blinked. "Huh?"

"Nothing. Just something I know." I pulled the gold-and-silver socks out of my pocket. "I go in and sniff the drawer about every day."

Janice sighed. "We're *so* sad."

"Yeah. She wouldn't like that I stole gold."

"She'd understand." Janice turned her face to the moon. "She always understood."

I put my hands over my face, and Janice's arms were around me. "I'm sorry I never help with the house stuff," she whispered. "I'm sorry I'm such a witch."

Well, that did it. A sob came out, couldn't help it, and then it was like every bad thing that happened in the last nine months exploded out of me and washed away. Janice's shirt got all wet.

"Cripes. What a hurricane," Janice said. But she kept her arms around me till I stopped hiccupping. Then she stood up and put the purple socks back in her pocket. "Let's go."

"Wait," I said. "Gotta check one thing." Because some

part of my mind had been worrying at that "biggest little house" thing Vilma said. And pixies.

I left Table Rock and found my way by moonlight to the biggest stone house, the one Mim helped me build by the rosebushes four years ago. There was an actual moonbeam on it, like it was daytime.

Something flicked past me, one side, then the other.

"What are you *doing?*" Janice said.

I knelt down and peered in the doorway. Something was in there, something big. Tied up with red string. It had pink flower petals scattered all over it.

It could've been a dead animal, but I was sure it wasn't. I hauled that thing out—it was burlap, heavier than it looked—untied the string, and shook a couple of the gold pieces out on the rock, gleaming in the moonlight.

Janice bent to look. "Is that what I think it is?"

Yes-s-s-s, the rapids said.

The burlap bag crinkled. I poked around inside and pulled out a piece of white paper, folded into a tiny square. Here's what it said: "Freely given. V."

Redemption.

I handed the note to Janice.

"It's a fuller bag than the one Vilma sold to Altin," I said. "Even Mim can't say this isn't enough to keep us here."

Something flitted past and I looked and . . . there he was. A two-inch guy in rags, covered in blue tattoos, sitting on the roof of the stone house my mom and I built.

He stood up and bowed. And—*flick!*—disappeared.

"Whoa," Janice said.

"Yeah," I said. "Finest kind."

Epilogue

The river is wide and calm in front of our house, and you hear the rapids all the time, a quarter mile around the bend. Here's what those rapids are telling you: Everything changes, but some things last forever. Keep moving and see where it takes you.

And if something flits past the corner of your eye . . . leave a candy bar.

RIVER RUNS FREE
David Windle

River runs free river runs free
along the rocky ridge and down
towards the sea
river runs free river runs free
like the wind and birds
and you and me.

As the slow sky turns
and the deep sun burns
and the dark earth
rests beneath
river runs free river runs free
like a glittering seam of stars.

As the leaves draw light
from the woven air
and the grass drinks hard
from the frozen soil
river runs free towards the sea
like a rope of silver silk.

As the quiet fish dive
and the birds alight
and the jungle
sings with life
river runs free with you and me
and the horizon calling endlessly.

Acknowledgments

The mysterious beast in Donna's river was born when Margaret Nevin and Emily Whiting, seventh graders at the time, fired up my imagination with a pair of stories they wrote at the Brooklin School. Hence the name "Margily." Thanks, you two.

Brooklin School kids fire up my imagination all the time, come to think of it. I'm grateful for the inspiration you give me every year.

Donna and crew were alternately informed and kept in line by insightful readers: Julia Baird, Lisa Heldke, Catherine Nevin, Gregory Maguire, Patricia McMahon, Becky Tapley, and of course Rob Shillady (four drafts this time). Shelly Perron was a godsend as usual. Phuc Tran and Peg O'Connor provided Latin advice while Chloé Johnson and Sergio Lee were naming consultants. I'm grateful for the advice of John Dennis and Mihku Paul-Anderson. And thank heavens for the hilarity and support of my writers' group: Kathleen Caldwell, Heidi Daub, Irene Eilers, Jean Fogelberg, Becky McCall, Gail Page, and Kim Ridley.

The mysterious beast would be in no river anywhere without genius editors Kathy Dawson and Rosie Ahmed.

A glittering seam of stars, in fact, to everyone at Dial, especially publisher Lauri Hornik, editorial director Nancy Mercado, production editor Regina Castillo, interior designer Jason Henry, jacket designer Maria Fazio, and cover illustrator Vivienne To. Dan Janeck is a stellar copy editor. Kudos to David Windle for the lovely "River Runs Free," which appears on PrimaryPoems.com, his website for budding poets and their teachers.

And Kate Testerman: Thanks for the sanity.